She for Her

a novel

RASHMI TRIVEDI

© **Rashmi Trivedi 2023**

All rights reserved

All rights reserved by author. No part of this publication may be reproduced, stored in a retrieval system or transmitted in any form or by any means, electronic, mechanical, photocopying, recording or otherwise, without the prior permission of the author.

Although every precaution has been taken to verify the accuracy of the information contained herein, the author and publisher assume no responsibility for any errors or omissions. No liability is assumed for damages that may result from the use of information contained within.

First Published in January 2023

ISBN: 978-93-5704-841-5

BLUEROSE PUBLISHERS
www.BlueRoseONE.com
info@bluerosepublishers.com
+91 8882 898 898

Cover Design:
Muskan

Typographic Design:
Tanya Raj Upadhyay

Distributed by: BlueRose, Amazon, Flipkart

Dedication

I salute you …

This book is dedicated to all the strong women, who have broken the stereotypes

and those who are still trying!

To name a few strong women in my life:

My mother Karuna: She was the first Hindu girl to graduate from her city. She also raised three strong, independent women

My sisters, Poonam and Jyoti: We always have each other's back.

My daughter Eshita: She too, proudly calls herself a 'feminist'.

My bestie, Irina: One of the strongest women, I know.

From my heart to yours...

From her birth till her death, a girl is given various instructions, most of which are made to suit the patriarchal system. Sit properly, talk softly, walk slowly, don't venture out alone, don't answer back, learn the household chores, etc. The list is endless. Then there are other narratives like, daughters are *paraya dhan*, women are weak, they are bad at math, they are too emotional to be rational, they are bad drivers, they are bad with money, and so on. These thoughts are implanted in her mind for a reason. To keep her in 'her place'!

It becomes so ingrained in her psyche, that she starts believing it to be true. Years of being brainwashed into believing that she was the weaker sex and that she needed to be 'protected' led her to believe that indeed she was.

However, she is now breaking the stereotypes, she is coming out of the so-called cocoon made for her and refusing to be cast into any mould. **She is negating the narrative!**

> *She is soft, but not malleable.*
> *She is emotional, but not gullible.*
> *She is strong and she is sharp,*
> *And she refuses to be selfless.*

Well, one such narrative that women have been fed is that "a woman is a woman's worst enemy."

Thereby ensuring that they always remain wary of each other and be at loggerheads. This was done to keep them busy fighting each other so that they do not unite to fight against the injustice meted out to them. How convenient for men!

Enough! It's time to break free from such limiting narratives. A woman is a woman's best friend. There is no greater bond than sisterhood. A woman understands, empathises, and supports women. After all, her struggles are the same, her challenges are common.

She is not her enemy. She is her friend. She is not competing with her, she is supportive of her.

Before being a daughter, sister, wife, mother, or mother-in-law, she is a woman.

And SHE is always FOR HER!

Foreword

Rashmi Trivedi is a prolific writer, and in the six years I have known her, she has penned six books, with this being her seventh. It has been my proud privilege as a friend to have read all six hitherto published books and now the seventh before it has so been.

As someone who has only written non-fiction, I am often amazed at how she can straddle writing fiction, non-fiction and poetry with equal ease.

She started as an author purely by chance when she had to live alone in Bhopal when Indian Oil, the organisation she works for, transferred her there. She did not want to take this assignment as she had never lived away from her family, who continued to stay in Delhi. However, the diffident Rashmi, who left reluctantly for Bhopal, not only learned to cope splendidly but also put down her experiences in 2016 in her first book called 'Woman everything will be fine'.

She returned to Delhi, a confident woman with the author in her unleased. She has since written three works of fiction in addition to this one and has also published two collections of poetry.

Her poetry deserves special mention, and my all-time favourite is 'My Dying Conscience', which went viral on the net and was plagiarised by many. There was a time when this poem kept coming back to me on many Whatsapp groups, with different poets claiming to have penned it. The climax was when it once came back as having been composed by Ram Jethmalani – after he had passed on!

All her books have had firmly etched female characters who transform themselves by unshackling themselves from dependencies and a diffident mindset to becoming strong and independent individuals, and this book is no exception.

The protagonist's idea of leaving her own house on discovering that her husband was leaving her for another woman, only so that the children don't miss their father, is the turning point that starts her on the path of discovering her inner strengths. The meeting with a younger man and the transformation from an employee perennially scared of her boss to a firebrand lawyer fighting for women's rights are very smoothly handled. The final pages, where she is once more pitted against the same challenges that tried to destroy her the last time, add a fine twist to the tale.

Rashmi's characterisation is, as usual, superb, and the characters mishmash beautifully to create a gripping tale. A great book to read and a fantastic author to follow. I have done the first and have been doing the second for a while now. Strongly recommend both!

Neelesh kulkarni

Entrepreneur, Theatre and voice-over artist, corporate coach, Author of 'In the footsteps of Rama- travels with the Ramayana', 'Where the Gods Dwell' and 'All India Radio- the great Unifier.'

I am so grateful…..

It was in 2020 that I came out with my last novel, " The lockdown". Even though my poetry collection "My dying conscience" was published in 2021, people kept asking me about my next novel.

So here it is, in your hands. SHE for HER - A book that tells the world that we women are NOT ready to believe and accept all the limiting narratives that are fed into our psyche.

This book is in your hands because:

1. Someone up there is always for me. He keeps me under His protection and that is all the protection I need. His blessings and mercies make my life joyous, blessed, and peaceful. He is in my thoughts, my words, and my pen. Eternally grateful to my Krishna and my Baba.

2. My parents are my source of strength. In my DNA , they also gave me empathy, creativity and sensitivity, all the qualities that are required to be a writer.

3. My husband is a feminist: Some men, love calling themselves feminists. My husband never claims to be one. His actions speak louder. In my house, there are no gender roles. I am so happy that my children will not have to " unlearn" anything. They have a role model to look up to, my husband! Also, this man is after my life when I am lazy and it was due to his constant nagging that this book is finally in your hands!

4. My children Eshan and Eshita look up to me: They are my first critic and give their honest feedback. The fact that they look up to me always makes me strive harder and give my best.

4. My friend and publisher, Syed always motivates: He rightly deserves a mention here. He is another person who motivates me to write. He also tells me that I should be present on social media. It was due to his persistence that I started posting reels and content on Instagram. From my first book to my seventh, I never felt the need to go to any other publisher. Syed, let me publicly acknowledge your support and tell you that I am forever indebted to you!

5. My readers' support: Last but not the least, I acknowledge your contribution to this book. The fact that this book is in your hands is motivation enough for me. Your feedback, your reviews, and your messages keep me going.

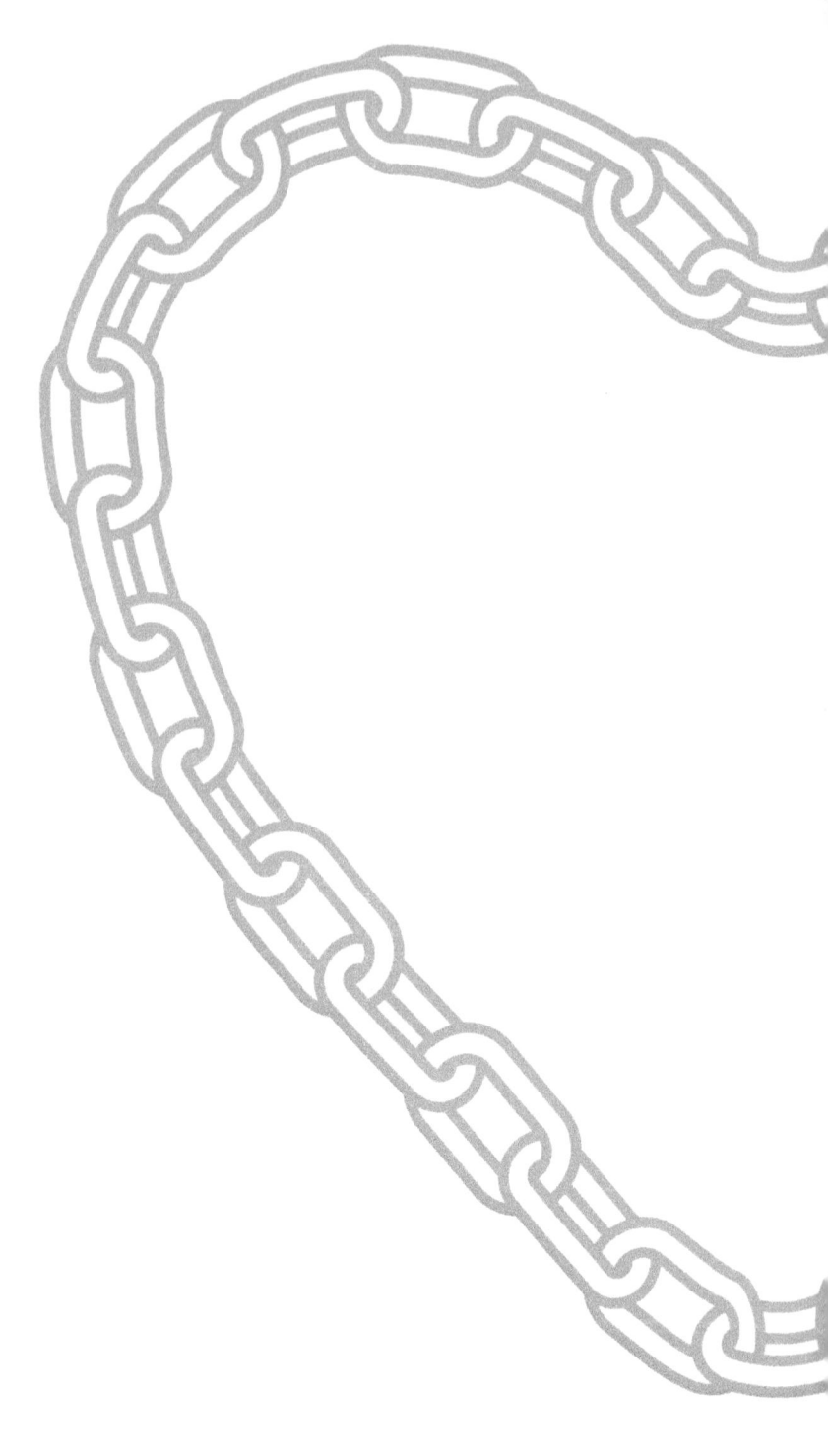

I t was just one of those days. Nothing had gone right since morning.

The alarm hadn't gone off for whatever reason and she had overslept; the constant ringing of the doorbell had woken her up. Sheetal looked at the clock. It was 6.30 AM! By now her breakfast should have been ready! It was the milk man who was ringing the bell. She jumped out of bed and rushed to open the door, quickly grabbing her robe and pulling it over her nightgown. Try as much not to, she was still very conscious of prying eyes that made her very uncomfortable. She used to feel that once she was older either people would stop staring or she would get used to the staring eyes but neither had happened.

She was nearing her fortieth birthday. God, she was old! How was it that she did not feel her age? She had never felt that she had grown up. People will laugh if they read her mind. Laugh? No, they would die of shock, she thought, and a soft smile played on her face as she opened the door and took the milk bottle from the milk man. Thinking that the smile was a greeting for him, the milk man got enthused. The robe, it seemed, did not make any difference as she felt his eyes linger on her cleavage. She gave him a stern look as she closed the door on him.

Today, there wouldn't be any time to make both lunch and breakfast. Breakfast would have to be cereal. The boys hated cereals, but they would have no choice today. It was better that they should be carrying lunch and not eat from the school canteen.

She put the milk to boil and rushed to the bathroom. No, today, she wouldn't have the time to scrutinize her face and count the fine lines that had already appeared and also look for the new ones which were eagerly waiting to make an appearance. She rushed through the morning routines as fast as possible, trying to multitask even in the bathroom. Of course, she could not help looking at her face in the mirror as she brushed her teeth.

She did not like what she saw. She saw a woman who looked ancient. She could never relate to the woman in the mirror. In her mind, she was still a beautiful young girl who always had a chain of admirers. She did not feel any different now. The truth was that she was far from young as far as appearances were concerned. Her hairline was receding. She wished for an app which could actually tell you the rate at which your hairline was receding. Oh, but that wouldn't help! She wished there was a miracle potion that would bring all the hair she had lost back to where it belonged overnight. "No, I don't want more; I am not greedy," she thought. "I just want whatever I had to return once again." She had beautiful hair, long, straight and silky. The only problem was that she kept losing her hair faster than she lost her spectacles or her keys. The face staring back at her from the mirror looked haggard to her.

The face which looked old and ancient to her was in reality, a face that anyone would look at twice. Sheetal, almost forty years old, was a beautiful female. What seemed like a receding hairline to her was a broad forehead with hardly any lines. Perhaps Sheetal's eyes had powerful lenses that could show the very fine lines to her, but in reality, no one would have guessed her to be a day over thirty. Talking of her eyes, they were big but not big enough to be mentioned in verses, and they were beautiful but not beautiful enough to set hearts aflutter. The only thing special about her eyes was that they were eloquent. Seriously, her eyes spoke a language of their own.

Her beautiful hair, expressive eyes, and dusky complexion made people think that she was a Bong. She was not. She was a typical Delhite. Her forefathers had migrated to Delhi from some remote corner of UP which she had never ever been to.

As she finished her routine morning chores in the washroom, she called out to her boys to wake up.

"Saurabh! Shashank! Get up, both of you. I don't have time to come to you ten times till you are awake. I am running late myself." She shouted from the washroom.

There was obviously no response from either of the boys, but she could hear a grunt coming from her own bedroom. Sanjay hated to be disturbed in the mornings, but there was no way she could wake up the boys by whispering into their ears nor could she stand in their bedroom and wait for them to finally decide to leave their beds. So, the usual routine was that she would keep calling out to them half an hour before the time that they should have been up so as to not miss the school bus. Most of the time, it would be Sanjay who would wake up before the boys, though he was the last one to leave home, and he would certainly not be in the best of moods.

As she did her superwoman act in the kitchen, her phone rang. The name on the screen had her literally sweating. It was Laxmi, her maid calling. A call from her, when she should have been here could mean only one thing. She was not coming today!

"Please, God, let her not say she is not coming. I honestly don't have the time to do the dishes or the sweeping," she prayed as she took her call. However, if God was on her side today, he would not have made her oversleep. He most certainly was not!

She made a mental note to do pooja or something to ensure she got into his good books again. She decided to do just a few dishes so that when her sons returned from school, they would have at least some plates to eat pizza from. She also decided to do away with the sweeping of the floor. 'I mean you can't have a spotlessly clean house and a five-star menu for lunch and dinner when you don't have a maid!' She thought.

She could visualize Sanjay making a face as he would find some dirt lying somewhere. But then, he had a knack for doing this even when the room was swept, mopped and made to shine so much that you could see your face in it. Sanjay would always end up finding some dirt even then. She would see the fine lines on his face even before they appeared since Sanjay always found something to complain about in the cleanest rooms!

Not that it bothered her any more. Initially, when she was a new bride and was all out to impress her newly acquired husband, she would actually sweep and mop the floor practically every time he would so much as glance at the floor with a frown. Sometimes she wondered if he did not like the unclean room or was it that he did not like to see her resting. Whatever it was, she would constantly be on her edge to keep the room clean.

Not anymore though. As much as she hated the thought of growing up and dreaded the thought of looking old, she also rejoiced at the confidence that her age had brought her. She could laugh at Sanjay when he would start off on his daily lectures about cleanliness. This would make him angrier, but she was not in awe of him anymore. There were no more impressions to create! He could very well get married to a *safai karamchaari* if he wanted a spotlessly clean house!

Sheetal was putting tadka in the dal when her phone rang again. She felt like screaming when she saw the name this time. "Dracula", it read. It was her boss. She kept aside the pan and took a deep breath before taking the call. Not taking the call would have been a bigger disaster. This would have ensured that Dracula drank every drop of her blood throughout the day. At least now he would only be sipping her blood for some time instead of taking big gulps.

"Sheetal, I hope you remember that we have our meeting. Mr. Shukla and his team are visiting today to discuss the way forward. I have only called to remind you about the meeting because you keep forgetting things these days and also to warn you that you dare not be late today." Dracula said at the other end.

Oh My God! That meeting was today! She had forgotten! She looked at the wall clock. There was no time. She had to rush.

She started to speak to herself. "How does it matter if you are late? You might lose this important client. So, how does that matter? You might lose the job. Did that matter?" She was not sure of that anymore. Once upon a time, when her career was very important to her, she had to compromise on her professional growth for the family's sake as her kids were very small. Now that they were not kids anymore, she felt that her ambition was inversely proportional to her age.

'Oh! I think I would enjoy preaching and giving sermons more than the business meetings that I attend,' she thought to herself. But the fate of God-men and God-women was not very bright these days so, she decided that she was better off with her business meetings.

How she worked in the next few minutes would have put Rajnikant to shame. It wasn't long after that she left the house with not only her lunch but also after having a packed lunch for Sanjay and the kids.

"As a new day starts, new opportunities will unfold.

I am Midas, I can turn every moment into gold."

She rhymed childishly, smiling to herself as she drove her car in the heavy traffic. She loved poetry and her subconscious mind would rhyme, which she would sometimes put on paper and sometimes not.

Today, she needed extra positivity to deal with Dracula as despite all her best efforts, she was going to be late for work.

Rohit got up before the alarm could ring. He knew that his body clock was better than any alarm clock. He just had to decide what time he had to be awake, and his eyes would open at that exact moment. The alarm clock too, started to ring. It was just out of sheer curiosity that he would put an alarm daily. It was a competition between him and the clock. Of course, he was winning since the clock had run out of battery on one occasion and failed to ring.

He pushed aside the comforter and jumped out of bed. This was the best part of the day. He loved the mornings, dawn to be precise. It was the time when the moon and the sun would both compete for a place in the sky! The moon would always lose and disappear into oblivion only to come out again at night and claim its rightful place amongst the stars.

He should seriously start writing more of poetry, he thought. He did not find time for the new book he had started to write so, finding time to write poetry was out of the question. But sometimes, he would think in verses. If only there was a mechanism by which all his thoughts could get converted into words automatically and flow into a word file on his desktop, he would have written a Broadway musical by now! He smiled at his thoughts.

He slept to see his dreams at night, he woke up to find his dreams in sight

Chasing them as a man possessed, he wouldn't give up, and used all his might.

He smiled at the rhyme that he had created in a jiffy. He loved doing this. It was his dream to write, direct and produce a musical.

Words and music were the two gifts God had bestowed on him for which he was grateful. Of course, his life had many blessings, but these two were close to his heart.

Rohit had spent all of his 27 years on this planet being in love with words and music. Ever since he was a little boy, he had been fascinated by music and poetry. His mother would say that he had learnt all the nursery rhymes even before learning the alphabets. In fact, he would make his own rhymes which would jingle even if they made no sense. He could catch any tune very fast. He would hum the tune of the advertisements on TV. Before he could speak, he had started singing! At least, this was what his mother had him believe since he was too young to remember himself!

How nice would it have been if he could remember his childhood days. He wanted to listen to that child who would make senseless rhyming jingles. He smiled at the thought. If he could have had his way, he would make sure that everyone spoke only in jingles. He laughed out aloud at this thought. This would actually ensure that people who spoke nonsense nonstop would speak less.

He hardly spent ten minutes in the wash room and was ready for his run. He slipped into his sneakers and strapped on his fitness band to track the run. After writing and music, running was the next best thing for him.

He took his usual path for the run and went to the running track, nearest to his apartment. It was a huge park with a broad track on the sides for running or walking. He had to run 3 kms from his home to reach there, but after that, it was a great place to be running in. There were some runners but mostly people who had come for a morning walk.

With the music playing and the body switching to the 'auto' mode for running, he felt his body craving for the ecstasy that came with stretching the body to its limit while running. At 6 feet 2 inches, he also had to be careful not to put on additional weight. He would look like a giant if he did that.

Rohit was an author, freelance content writer, digital marketeer, and a professional guitarist during his free time. Of course, playing the guitar professionally was not something he got to do very often these days. He played with a band in which a very close friend was the vocalist. The band was doing well, but he often found himself backing out of performances due to work pressure.

Rohit was originally from Rajasthan, even though his family had settled in Guwahati for many years now. His grandfather had come from a village in Rajasthan and had started trading in spices. Very soon he opened a shop and the business grew. His father and uncle got into partnership, and they soon started trading in other grocery items . The business was doing well, and he was also expected to join after he graduated from Cotton College, but he had other plans. He joined a course in digital marketing, and at the same time, started using it to promote the family business. The results were astounding, and this gave him the confidence to do it for other companies of families and friends. Soon his passion became his work, and he decided to try his luck in Delhi.

It was two years ago, that he had landed in Delhi with dreams in his eyes and fire in his belly. He had rented an apartment in Greater Kailash and started his company afresh. Initially, through contacts but gradually through word of mouth and his marketing efforts business started pouring in so much so, that he had to hire two people to help him with the work. When he was growing slowly but steadily, he wrote an inspirational book, "The fire Within You." Though the book was not a financial success, but the younger generation appreciated it. Companies had started to invite him to conduct workshops on digital marketing, and he was often invited to colleges to give lectures on how to become young entrepreneurs.

"Life has been good," he thought to himself as one foot fell on the pavement, followed by the other at a rhythmic speed. He started to get the high that he could not get from any stimulant other than running!

The shrill noise of the alarm brought Richa back into the world from the dreamland she was floating in. She did not want the dream to end. She was at a party, and a handsome hunk was vying for her attention. She had just agreed to dance with him when her mobile rang. It wasn't her mobile which had woken her up but the alarm clock. It felt as if she had fallen onto the cement of harsh reality with a thud from the magical dreamland of her fantasy. She wanted that dance with that man.

'*Let me try to sleep for some more time,*' she thought as she took another pillow and put it on top of her head, and at the same time, shutting off the alarm of her phone with the other hand.

Reality takes seconds to sink in. It seeps through the tiniest of cracks and then hits you hard. In a fraction of a second, Richa realized that the dance would have to wait for some other night. Today, she was slated for an interview with an advertising company. The interview was at ten, and she would have to hurry to be on time. She threw the cover off the bed and jumped out.

It was eight in the morning and too early by her standards. Richa loved to sleep till noon waking up only to eat lunch. Her day would begin only after that. But her fun days were going to end soon. She had taken a break for a few months after graduation to travel and do everything she had always wanted to do. She had joined a self-defense class and also a pottery class. The clay running through her hands and getting molded into beautiful shapes was strangely very therapeutic. It made her feel in control as if she had the power to shape the destiny of the pieces in her hands.

If she wanted, she could make a beautiful plate that would adorn the wall of a happy home or she could make a *surahi* that would lie in the corner of a *jhuggi* quenching the thirst of the labors when they would return home after a hard day's work under the sun; She could make a diya to be lighted in a temple or a vase to be adorned with colorful flowers; She could create toys for children to play with or a *gullak* to store money. It was her choice and her decision to make whatever she wanted to. This gave her a sense of power and self-worth.

Very soon, she would have to organize an exhibition of her work. She had made a beautiful collection of artistic pottery. She was an artist at heart. She had no idea why on earth she had done BBA. Perhaps because she did not want to be an engineer or a doctor, the next best thing everyone was doing was taking a degree in business management. She planned to work for a few years, gain some experience and then opt for doing MBA from some reputed institute.

It was her father's idea that she should apply for a job in an advertising company. He spoke to someone and arranged for an interview with the company. Richa was not very happy with all this, but she did not complain. After all, she got to do many things as per her wish. So it did not matter if her parents interfered in her life now and then. Both her parents were doctors, and they wanted her to study medicine too. Richa had put her foot down and declared that she would not do either medicine or engineering. They settled for her to do BBA so that she could do MBA from a foreign university to get a good job.

Her parents lived in a small industrial city called Haldia where they were employed in Hindustan Levers. After completing her schooling from a small town, doing graduation in Kolkata was the obvious choice as it was the nearest metro city. Richa again insisted that she wanted to study college in Delhi. The city had always fascinated her. Despite all the horror stories about the city being unsafe that she had read or heard, it remained alluring for her. Maybe it fascinated her because it was unsafe and risky! Richa had a reckless trait in her. She knew it. So, when she insisted that she wanted to graduate from a college in Delhi, her parents had to relent. She was admitted to Shaheed Sukhdev College of Management Studies, one of the best colleges in Delhi for BBA. During her first year in college, she stayed in the college hostel but later took a paying guest accommodation near the campus.

After joining the company, she intended to shift somewhere in south Delhi because the company's office was in Nehru Place.

As she rushed through the daily chores, she frowned. True, her father had put in a word for her to the company's General

Manager, but that did not mean she could take liberties. She had to be punctual and she needed to hurry.

The previous night, she had ironed and laid down the clothes that she would be wearing. She had chosen a smart crème-colored Allen Solly shirt paired with tan-colored trousers. She had also selected her brown stilettos to go with it. High heels always gave a confidence boost. It is funny how sometimes small things make a difference in your mood. Smart pencil heels always sky-rocketed her mood, that, along with a chic bag, of course!

As she came out of the washroom in a towel and reached out for her shirt, she noticed something on it. Just beneath the collar, there was a hole, not a neat hole but a hole with rugged corners. No! She screamed inwardly; it was that damn rat again. She would have to do something about that damned Rat!

Meanwhile, she would have to wear something else. She rummaged through the cupboard and looked for another shirt that would go with her trousers. Her shirts were crumbled into balls. While some were dirty and had been kept aside for washing others were washed but not ironed. '*I better get organized,*' she told herself as she ironed another crème-coloured shirt.

She wore her clothes as quickly as she could, picked up her bag and rushed out of the flat. She tried to book an Ola but none was available. It was the same when she tried to book an Uber. It was difficult to get any cabs during peak hours.

She hailed an auto and asked, "*Bhiaya, Nehru Place chalenge?*"

The auto driver looked at her with lewd eyes and then shook his head in denial. Tears of helplessness welled up in her eyes!

She looked at her watch! She should have been in the office by now. 'Damn! I will be late on the first day of my work!' She felt like screaming in frustration, but she quietly hailed another auto.

Sheetal noted the time as she quietly entered the office. It was 9.30 and she was late by 30 minutes. She walked to her room with a straight face and trying to make the least sound. Dracula's room was next to hers, and she had to go past the room to reach hers. She fervently hoped he would not notice her, but that was not to be. Nancy, his secretary, sat in a cubicle outside his room, greeted her in the loudest possible voice.

"Good morning, Sheetal ma'am," she smiled at her. "Good morning, Nancy," Sheetal replied with a smile that could have frozen the water that Nancy was sipping!

She hoped that Dracula would be dozing and would not have heard the conversation outside his room, but this was not her lucky day.

"Sheetal, please come to my room," he called out to her. "Yes Sir, in a minute," she replied as she barged into her room and threw her bag on the side table. She picked up her pen and her diary but as she was about to go out, she stopped. She took a few long breaths, breathe in... breathe out. She was reading a book where it was mentioned that such breaths helped control stress. With a smile and a positive attitude, she went into her Boss's room.

Dracula was sitting on his chair, his bulky body barely fitting in. She had often wondered why he would not order a new chair.

Did he not want his entire body to be seated? On this chair, at least 20 % of his body, in various shapes, protruded from the sides. His legs were stretched out in front of him. They were surprisingly very lean as compared to the body. His structure gave an impression of a big lollipop, Sheetal thought as she tried to suppress her smile. She had this stupid knack of smiling at the wrong time, which often got her into trouble.

She had failed to hide her smile on time, and Dracula had caught it before she could pull up a straight face.

"Mrs. Sheetal Chopra, are you laughing at me, because like a fool, I am in the office before time, preparing for today's meeting where as you are late by 30 minutes?" Dracula pointed at his watch as he made this statement. He could be very sarcastic when he wanted, and he would always address people by their full names whenever he was annoyed.

This was certainly not a good sign, and before it got out of hand, she had to put things right.

"Sorry Sir, Shashank was not feeling well so, I had to take him to the hospital," she lied through her teeth. After years of working with him, she knew that telling the truth was never an option with him. He would not be pacified if she had said that she had overslept or that the maid had not come. When it came to her duty towards her children and husband, he would suddenly soften his stand and stop persecuting her. He was one of those men who thought that a woman's place was at home, and that a working woman was usurping a job that was rightfully a man's. Some poor man somewhere deserved and needed this job more than her, and by working, she had denied him the opportunity.

'*Well, not only he, but most of the men like to see women at the office only as secretaries or in other junior positions,*' she thought grimly as she tried putting up her best "damsel in distress" face which worked with her boss.

She noticed that he mellowed down a bit.

"Yes, the weather is changing, and children do tend to fall sick. As a mother, it's your duty to take care," he said looking at her with accusing eyes as if she was a convict standing in front of a judge who was forced to acquit her when in fact, he wanted to convict her.

"Yes sir," she said as she sat down across the table.

"Mr. Shukla and his team will be arriving at ten thirty today. We have only an hour to discuss our strategy." She noticed that he was still in a complaining mood. '*Perhaps my face wasn't pathetic enough.* I should join an acting class,' she thought and again suppressed a smile.

"Sir, my presentation is ready. I will take you through it," she said and within seconds she was all professional. She discussed her action plan for Mr. Shukla's company for the next twenty minutes.

Mr. Shukla was a self-made man who had started his business when he was in college. He was into the business of spices. He mainly exported in foreign markets and was planning to enter the domestic market in a big way.

Sheetal's company, Bright Marketing Solutions was into advertising and marketing. The director of the company, Mr. Paricker had passed on this lead to them, and they were trying to convert this lead into business. After many follow-ups, Mr.

Shukla finally agreed for a business meeting to discuss the plan they had come out with. Today, he will be coming for a detailed discussion regarding this project.

Sheetal was given charge of the project, and she had been working on it for the previous two weeks. She knew it was expected of her to get the deal. She had had many meetings with Mr. Shukla which had gone very well. It was then informed to them that Mr. Shukla had appointed a Marketing Consultant, and that he would be handling the project on their behalf. She was ardently hoping that they would be able to close the deal that day and begin working on it.

Sheetal was a very creative person, and she knew that this was her strength. Even though there were others devoting more time and effort in the company, she would always end up putting up the best proposals. The clients selected her ideas, but when it came to the execution part, she lagged behind in getting the job done. The pressure of the industry was such that it demanded you to work at ungodly hours, and you were at the beck and call of the client. This was where she lacked. She had several other things to do other than just pleasing the clients!

She had a husband and two young boys to look after. Till the previous year, she also had a father-in-law. He had passed away eight months ago. He was against having a full-time help at home, so she also had to do the cooking herself. She had tried reasoning with him many times, but he was stubborn as a bull when it came to having his way. '*Like father, like son,*' she would think.

She sometimes feared that her sons would also be like them. Thankfully, this had not happened, yet. Sheetal would prepare breakfast and Lunch for all of them and, after returning from work, cook dinner. Her father-in-law often complained that he had to heat the food himself and that the food kept in the fridge never tasted as good as freshly made food. Of course, she had always turned a deaf ear to all the complaints. There was a limit to how much a person could do. If you wanted the "*Laxmi*" of the house to bring in "*Laxmi*", then you had to be prepared to make small sacrifices!

Now with her father-in-law gone, she had tried to broach the subject of having a full-time domestic help, but now it was Sanjay who dissuaded her. She noticed that the respite, which she should have gotten from her father-in-law's barbs after his passing away, was now being compensated by Sanjay having replaced his father. She had read about females turning cranky as they age, but she did not know that men became worse. When she had got married, her mother-in-law was alive, and contrary to what everyone said about mothers-in-law, hers was a true gem. Sanjay often took up the role of a typical mother-in-law, often finding faults with whatever she did. Initially it used to upset her, and she would cry more often than laugh. Things did not improve even after the birth of the boys. Later, she realized that it was in his nature to be critical of everyone and everything. No one could match his expectations. He was a perfectionist, and even though he was far from being perfect, he expected it from others.

As the years passed, Sheetal learned to ignore him and do things the way she wanted. His bickering did not change with time; she only got used to them. He was a good husband despite his nature. He was often considerate, not expressive, but he would fulfill all his duties. He was good to her parents and brother. He never objected to her spending money on herself. He did not even bother to find out how much money she earned. Perhaps that was because he knew her earnings would be more than his. Once she adjusted to his nature, Sheetal found life easy. *'Life is peaceful when you make peace with the chaos of your life,'* she thought.

Suddenly the intercom rang. It was Dracula. "Sheetal," he said. "I forgot to mention that a new intern will be joining us today. She is the daughter of one of Mr. Chattrejee's friends. I have told her to meet you at ten sharp. I am attaching her with you to work on the Shukla case. Brief her and bring her to the meeting with the client."

Mr. Chattrejee was a general manager looking after vendor development and strategy planning. He was not fond of her and vice versa. Somehow, she felt that their stars did not match.

When you are already hard-pressed for time, having an intern working with you is a pain rather than a help. They are raw and have to be explained everything. They have to be trained and who has that kind of time to train interns? She grimaced inwardly. This day certainly wasn't going very well. An intern was loaded on her who had come with the recommendation of her arch-enemy in the company! What could get worse?

It was already ten. Where was the girl? She needed to brush up on her presentation before the client arrived. She did not have time, and if she went into the meeting without briefing her or without her all together, she would be in trouble.

Richa sighed! Nothing had gone right since morning. After finding that her favorite shirt had become food for a despicable rodent, she had failed to find a cab. After refusal by many auto drivers, she had finally found one. When she had reached Nehru Place and got out of the auto and walked just a few steps the heel of her shoe came off! She was literally in tears as she searched for a cobbler to mend the heel. Finally, when she reached office, it was ten minutes past eleven.

The office of Bright Marketing Solutions was on the fifth floor of a prominent building in Nehru Place. As she reached the lift lobby of the building, she saw that one of the lifts had just stopped at that floor. She rushed towards it to ensure it did not leave without her. She was in such a hurry that she did not see the person coming from the other side who was also trying to get into the lift. They bumped into each other, and the file that she was carrying in her hands fell onto the floor. That was the last straw! The tears which were just swimming in her eyes now decided to venture down to her cheeks, and she burst out crying.

With the tears in her eyes, she did not see the face of the person she had bumped into, but she realized that the person had bent down and was picking up the papers scattered all around the floor.

As he got up to hand over the papers to her, he noticed her tear-streaked eyes, and a look of sympathy crossed his face.

"I am really sorry. I did not mean to bump into you, but I am sure this is not such a catastrophe that you should cry as if the world has ended," he said, looking at her.

"Was he mocking her?" Richa wondered. She squeezed her eyes tight to clear her vision. Through her tears, she saw a face that belonged to a man in his late twenties, perhaps. He was not mocking her, for he had a very understanding look on his face.

His eyes were so kind that he need not have spoken anything, and she would have known that he was trying to help her. That gentle smile playing on his face was undoubtedly not derisive.

"Well, it is just that nothing has gone right since morning, and I am very late for my first day at work," she spoke spontaneously.

'God! Why did she have to tell all this to a stranger!" She thought to herself.

"Oh! One of those days!" He nodded at her sympathetically. "Let us not delay you further," he said as he pointed towards the lift, which had arrived again.

"Which floor," he asked.

"Fifth," she said.

He looked at her and smiled. "I am also going to fifth. I am Rohit," he said as he extended his hands formally.

"Richa," she said as she shook his hands. His handshake was gentle yet firm.

They arrived on the fifth floor and found that there was only one office on that floor, that of Bright Marketing Solutions.

They smiled at each other as they went towards the reception together.

Richa spoke first.

"I am Richa. I have come to join as an intern," she told the receptionist.

"Oh! Finally!" The receptionist sighed. "Please go and meet Sheetal ma'am. She had called up twice to enquire if you had come. She has to go for a meeting so hurry! Her room number is 21. It is straight down this corridor," she told her pointing towards her left.

Richa turned back to look at Rohit who was looking at her with the same friendly smile.

"Bye," she said. "It was nice meeting you."

"Bye," he said. "Though I have a feeling we will be meeting again soon."

Richa was puzzled at his reply, but she was in too much of a hurry to ponder over it. She rushed towards room number 21 to meet her new boss who had already enquired about her twice!

As she was about to enter the room, she stopped and decided to use the washroom to freshen up first. She was sure she looked disheveled with her tear strained face, and she wanted to create a good impression. '*A few minutes would not matter*,' she thought as she went towards the ladies' room. It did not take her even five minutes, and she was back in front of room number 21. She knocked on the door softly and heard a female voice answer.

"Come in."

She walked in with a bright smile, trying to bring gaiety in her voice when in reality, she was tense.

The lady across the table looked anything but happy. She was not pleased with something. '*Of course! It must be because of I am late,*' she thought.

"Good Morning Ma'am. I am Richa. My apologies for being late." God! This was not a good way to introduce yourself.

"Good Morning Richa. Please take a chair. Meet Mr. Rohit, a consultant for M/S Shukla & Co." She pointed to the person seated on a chair across her table.

That was when she noticed him.

"Oh! Hello," she said.

"We met at the lift." He told her boss. In fact, we had a minor accident, and it delayed her."

"Oh! I hope none of you is hurt," she asked.

"I am fine." They both replied at the same time.

Richa was grateful to him for having skillfully provided an excuse on her behalf for being late. Bumping wasn't exactly an accident, but a little exaggeration never harmed anyone!

Richa sat down on a chair beside him.

"Well, I would have liked to brief you about this project beforehand, but since there isn't time now, I will explain after the meeting. You have been assigned to me for this project. Mr. Shukla was also supposed to come for this meeting, but since he could not make it, he has sent his consultant for discussions." The frown on her face gave away the fact that Mr. Shukla's actions hadn't exactly thrilled her.

She glanced at Rohit and said, "I was hoping to close this today as there is a lot to be done if we have to meet the target date, but I guess in his absence, we will not be able to finalize the deal."

"Ma'am, Mr. Shukla has left the decision to me. If your proposal interests me, we will close the deal today. Mr. Shukla will look after the financial aspect after I approve the creative proposal." Even though he tried not to sound like he was boasting, to Richa, it did sound as if he was trying to flex.

She also had asked for it by doubting his capabilities and complaining about Mr. Shukla's absence.

Sheetal was quick to recover. "That's great then. It's always advantageous when you have to show the proposal to a creative mind. It needs a creative person to understand and appreciate creative work."

Was she trying to oil the young man, Richa was amused. One moment she sounded condescending and the next she was smooth when she knew that was the decision-making authority.

"Let's all go to the small conference room where I will prepare our proposal presentation. My boss, Mr. Subramaniam will join us," she said and moved towards the door.

The meeting, which she had thought would be over in an hour or so, lasted well past the lunch hour. Sheetal had suggested breaking for lunch, but Rohit had not wanted to break the flow of discussions, which was the right thing to do. Richa was a silent spectator. She was smart enough to understand that this was not an educational tour for her and that she was actually on the battlefield. Dracula had an urgent call from a client where something had gone wrong, so he apologized and left before they could even begin the presentation. So, it was only the three of them in the conference hall.

Sheetal shared a few of her ideas for the campaign, and Rohit had shown keen interest in all of them, asking the right questions. After working in this field for many years and giving presentations to many clients, she had now come to know when the client was sold to a particular idea. She could decipher the "this is it!" look on her client's face that was not yet seen on Rohit's face. Though she could see that he had more than "liked" a few ideas, she still wanted the client to be "in love" with the idea. Liking is a compromise. Love stays.

She was now on her last idea. She had saved the best for the last. With trepidation, she shared this, hoping to see the spark in his eyes.

The concept was a little sexual, but then, sex sells! The theme was that a young couple, who had been married for a few years, found that their sex life had become boring. So, they experimented with different fantasies to spice up their sex life. The jingle went something like this

To spice up your mood, be naughty, not nice

To spice up your food, just add SAC spice

As she discussed her plan for this particular idea, the look in his eyes told her that this deal was done. She could see that he was in love with this idea!

She completed her presentation, and to her surprise, she found the new girl, Richa clapping.

"Ma'am, all your ideas were great," she said, speaking for the first time in hours.

"Thanks Richa, and I hope Rohit also likes them." She said, looking at him for his response.

"I agree with the intern," he said. "I would also like to add that I absolutely loved the last one. Sex sells in India like nothing does."

"True." Sheetal said, hoping that Rohit would say something about closing the deal.

"I think we have a winner here, but please give me some time. I would like to sleep over it and will get back to you with my decision in a day or two.

Sheetal was disappointed! Nothing had been going right since morning, and she should have known she would not be clinching the deal today. Still, she had a good chance of getting this business. She was professional enough not to let her disappointment show.

"Sure Mr. Jain, we are in no hurry. Please take your time." Sheetal said, smiling at her client, but her formal address conveyed to him her disappointment

Sheetal invited him to lunch, which he declined, saying he had an urgent meeting and had to rush.

Sheetal saw him off and then told Richa to have lunch in the cafeteria and later go to the HR department to complete the joining formalities.

Dracula had not come back, so she left a message informing him that the deal could not be closed. She could imagine him scowling when he read this and was sure that the moment he was free, he would certainly call her to show his displeasure.

Sheetal went to her room and sat down on her chair. She looked at the wall clock and grimaced. It was already 2.30. The kids would be home by now. She should have called up to check, but she had completely forgotten. Sanjay would have called and certainly asked if Mumma had called. In the evening, he would pass a remark, something like, "They are your children and not your neighbors'."

It was different for him. Sanjay worked in a multinational firm and was placed in a senior position. He had a personal attendant who would remind him of things. Moreover, he was in the Finance department where the pressure mounted only when a quarter ended or the year ended. But for her, it was different. She was continuously under pressure to perform. It was a private firm, and the employee's output had to be much more than the company's cost.

She called home. There was no reply. She then called up on Saurabh's mobile. The phone was busy. Her elder son's mobile was always busy these days! She was sure he had a girlfriend or perhaps many girlfriends. She was not sure how it worked with the youngsters these days.

She then called up Shashank. He picked up after a few rings.

"Yeah Mom," he said. "Aunty has not come today?" Sheetal could hear the excitement in his voice. This meant Pizza for them.

"No, and because I did not know she would not be coming, I could not cook anything for you." Sheetal was felt guilty even though she knew that the kids would be happier eating pizza.

Of course, Sanjay would certainly make a scathing comment on the unhealthy eating habits of their children.

"Yippee!" Shashank yelled with glee. "I will ask bhaiya to place an order on swiggy," he said and kept the phone down not bothering to listen to what Sheetal had to say.

Sheetal sighed as she heard the beep on the phone of the disconnected call. She heard her stomach rumbling, reminding her that she had not eaten anything since morning. She called up canteen services and asked for a coffee and sandwich.

As she took the first bite of her sandwich, her phone rang. It was Dracula. She took a deep breath and kept the sandwich down as she took the call.

"Sheetal, why was the deal not closed? Will you miss this account also?" was the first thing that he said. The words cut through her heart like an arrow. He was referring to the Lalwani's account which had slipped from her hand the previous month. She had categorically told Dracula why the business was lost. The owner of the company, Mr. Rajat Lalwani, was a man in his fifties and had personally been negotiating the deal.

They had opened a new education center and needed to build the brand name. Two other companies had also quoted for the same business, but Sheetal's advertising plan was very creative, and she was sure to get the business. During the initial meeting, she realized that Mr. Lalwani was showing undue interest in her. She was used to it. Being a woman in the competitive corporate world was not easy. People think that if you are ambitious, you are also available. She had handled many such cases with tact and diplomacy. She had ruffled quite a few feathers which had never been a major issue.

But it had been different that time. It was customary that they take the key person of the client out for lunch or dinner. Many customers liked to be wined and dined. Sheetal preferred to go out for lunch rather than dinner. She also managed to do dinner sometimes, but she always ensured that she took along some other colleague with her. Mr. Lalwani had insisted for dinner when she had offered to meet for lunch on a Saturday. She, somehow, did not feel comfortable with him. It was her womanly instinct though he had not behaved inappropriately with her. Till that night, that is.

That night they had gone to the Marriot Hotel in Saket. She was with her colleague, Sarthak who was her junior and was working on the same account. They were having drinks when after a few pegs, Mr. Lalwani had said that he wanted to show them some designs and that the same was in a file he had forgotten in the car. He had given the car keys to Sarthak to get them from the car. As soon as Sarthak had left, his tone changed. He looked at her with lustful eyes and said, "Sheetal, do you know that you are an extremely sexy woman? I get a hard on just looking at you." Sheetal had been shocked!

"How dare you talk to me like that Mr Lalwani?" She fumed.

"I am only being honest with you. I am sure you know this. Looking at your figure, no one can say that you are a mother of two teenage boys." He had stared leeringly at her cleavage. "Mr. Ramaswamy is a lucky bastard to have such a hot woman working *under* him." He had stressed the word "under" and laughed at his joke.

'Did he think that she was having an affair with Dracula?' Sheetal had been furious and was about to get up when Sarthak had returned, unaware of the undercurrents.

"Sarthak, I will have to go. There is an emergency at home." She had told him and then excused herself and left the room.

The next day, she requested Dracula to remove her from the Lalwani account. She had told him about the incident but had toned it down a bit, not mentioning Lalwani's innuendo about their relationship.

He had been thoughtful for a while, frowning and thinking.

"Sheetal, it is a major account for us, and we need it badly. I could give it to someone else, but I don't have the same confidence in anyone else I have on you. You are not a teenager; You are a mature woman, and I am sure you will be able to handle this."

Sheetal had been quiet. 'He was right. She had to handle it herself. If she ran scared at such incidents, she would be unable to work.'

During the next few meetings, she ensured she was never left alone with Lalwani. On a fateful day, they were in a meeting in his room when Sarthak had got a call from home and had to leave immediately. She had been left in the room alone with him. She had braced herself in case he said anything indecent. They were sitting beside each other on the sofa, looking at the artwork on the table in front of them. Before she could have realized what had happened, he had bent forward and kissed her on her lips and his hands had reached for her breasts.

Sheetal was left immobile. She had heard of molestation, but this had never happened to her. Her limbs had refused to move, her heart had stopped beating.

"I have wanted to kiss those sexy lips for a long time. Sheetal, it was your sexy lips that won this business for your company. You tell Mr. Ramaswamy that." The voice sounded as if it came from far.

Sheetal could not believe what had just happened. 'Did this man really think that her company employed her for the sexual gratification of the customers?'

She had slowly come out of her shocked state and found strength in her limbs.

"Mr. Lalwani, there is one small thing I want to tell you," she said as she stood up.

"Yes, yes, please say it." His thoughts might have been that the chick was just a few steps away from his bedroom, so he had also gotten up from the sofa.

She had moved a little on the side, pulled her right arm backwards, garnered all her strength and slapped him hard on the cheeks! This time it was his turn to be shocked, and Sheetal had taken this opportunity to flee from the scene.

Surprisingly, she had not been furious after that. The slap, which had taken all her strength, made her feel very good and relieved.

'He will carry the marks of my fingers on his cheeks for a few days at least,' were her thoughts as she had hurried down the stairs in a euphoric mood.

Only when she was in her car did the realization of what had happened sink in. She had gone straight to home and texted Dracula that she was not feeling well.

She had a sinking feeling at the pit of her stomach the entire day. She had felt unclean and tainted. She had washed her lips a hundred times, and yet she could feel the remains of his sloppy kiss on her lips. She had somehow felt responsible. Perhaps she had led him on by not making it clear that she was not interested in his advances. Perhaps she had smiled too much. Perhaps her dressing style had been wrong. Sanjay often complained that she went to the office as if going for a beauty pageant. But then, she was used to him finding faults with whatever she did. Sheetal had always been fond of good clothes and make-up. She would dress up even if she had to go to the market. She always felt more confident dressed up. Her clothes were not exorbitantly priced, but they were all very stylish and modern. She had her own style and never bothered about the current fashion.

Today she was starting to have doubts about her appearance. Was she unconsciously 'inviting" trouble? Why did she always have to face such unwanted attention even at this age? Sanjay kept on telling her that she should "dress her age" but then, *she did not feel old!*

Sanjay could make out that she was very restless and asked her why. She did not say anything. She knew that he would certainly blame her, and she was unsure how he would react towards the incident. He might also ask her to quit her job. Sometimes, she wished they were friends instead of husband and wife. How nice it was for couples who were more of friends than spouses. She felt like talking to her only friend in the world, Milli but she was travelling .

She could not sleep that night and wondered how to break the news to Dracula. The next day, when she reached the office, she was summoned to his room.

"It's over," he said. "What did you say to Mr. Lalwani? He has terminated our contract. I got this message yesterday night. He wants nothing to do with us anymore." He said in a grim voice. Then without waiting for her answer, he said, "I can guess what must have happened, but obviously, you could not handle it maturely without harming the company. Tell me Sheetal, why does the company have to pay the price of you being an attractive woman? This business was ours, but now we have lost it because of you."

Sheetal remained in a state of shock for the next two days. *'At this rate I will have a heart attack soon,'* she thought.

With that attitude, she did not find any reason to explain things to him. A working woman is alone in this world of wolves, and no number of laws actually makes it easy for her. Law can only help you take action, but who wants this kind of publicity anyway! No law could teach her how to deal with such a situation.

Dracula had not spoken to her normally for weeks, and today, yet again, he had referred to that incident, indirectly reminding her that she was under scrutiny and that she better secure the business.

'Sometimes,' she thought, 'whatever we may say about equality, the fact remains that women and men are never on the even playing ground. A woman has to fight a thousand battles for the same thing that comes to men as their right.'

She felt like a doe amongst a cackle of hyenas. She could only rely on her brains to survive the modern jungle where people were ready to pounce on her the moment, she let her guard slip.

The coffee on her table had gone cold, and she no longer felt like eating the sandwich. The new intern was at the door, asking her if she should come later.

"Come in," she said, gathering herself back again. She had to fight back if she had to survive. Her only ammunition were her skills and the capability to work hard. She knew that she would succeed!

What a day it had been! Richa sighed. Even though nothing had gone right since morning, she knew it was a day she would remember throughout her life. For the first time in her life, she had met a man who had set her heart aflutter. She was not one to believe in love at first sight. In fact, she found the idea utterly stupid.

Also, she was not new to relationships. She had two broken relationships behind her. One affair had lasted for three years – from the time that she was in class X to the time that she had been in class XII. The boy had been her senior, and they had dated in a place like Haldia. They would walk by the riverside and had also kissed behind the trees. They broke up when she moved to Delhi. Long distance affects the strongest of bonds, and theirs was just teenage romance. Neither of them was heartbroken!

The next relation that she had with a boy was a serious one in college. They were a gang of five, two boys and three girls. One of the boys, Mihir was silent and shy compared to the other boy, Gagan. So, she was more comfortable talking to Gagan. She always liked Mihir better though and would often wonder why he was not so open with her. She took it as a chalenge and made it a point to draw him into the conversations. Gradually, he opened up with her, and then there was no stopping him. He opened his heart to her and would consult her for anything and everything.

Then, one day, he declared his love for her. She was caught off guard as she had not expected this. She had asked for some time during which she had done some soul searching. She liked Mihir. No, she more than "liked" him. She was attracted to him and did not know where it would take her if she let herself lose. She said, 'yes'. They started dating and everything was fine.

After nearly a year, she realized that he was too possessive about her and did not give her space. But then, he loved her to the degree of madness. He kept on telling her that he would not be able to bear it if she broke up with him.

She was in a dilemma. She knew he was not right for her, but she did not know how to say this to him. The person that she had known as a friend and the person that he had become as a boyfriend were completely different. Nearly a year passed before she gathered courage to tell him their relationship was not working. It happened unexpectedly.

One day Gagan wanted some notes from her which were lying in her room, and so she invited him to her pad. He had a headache, and she gave him a disprin and offered to make tea. He agreed and lay down on her bed while she made tea. Just then the doorbell rang, and she answered it to see Mihir standing there. When he saw Gagan there, he did not say anything, but he was livid. He made some excuse and left.

Later, that day, they met in their usual café. A fight ensued, and he said he did not expect other men to go to her room! That was the last straw.

"I don't even give my parents the right to dictate to me. What I do or I don't is entirely my choice. I am breaking off with you. I have waited for a long time but did not dare to break off with you. I am sorry but I want out," she said and walked out of the restaurant.

It was a bad phase that they both went through after that. She had to deal with guilt and he with heartbreak. They say time is the best healer, and it made things better after some time. This incident made her very cautious. She did not want to get into any relationship. She was very honest with the guys with whom she went out on dates. "No relationship" was her mantra. At least, not till someone could make made her forget the mantra. Till date, no one had been able to do that.

There was something about that man, Rohit. He was a handsome dude, but that was not what drew her to him. It was his approach, his gentleness, the way he helped her to pick up the papers, the way he made her feel at ease, and the way that he looked at her with genuine concern. All these had added up to create an impression on her! No, she was not only impressed by him but she was also attracted to him.

She wanted to meet him again. She would, if they got the business. She fervently hoped that they did. She liked her boss also, although she did not talk much with her. 'She is an old lady, must be in her forties. She must have been beautiful when she had been young,' she mused. Her mom was 45 but she looked much older. 'Working women maintain themselves well,' she thought. 'I will never quit working even after marriage, if at all I marry, that is.' She smiled at her own thought.

She had gone to her boss after she finished her lunch in the company canteen. She had told her to go to the HR department and complete the formalities for joining the company. She had also said that she would introduce her to everyone in her team the next day. She looked troubled, and perhaps she was upset that the deal was not closed after the presentation. She looked desperate to close the deal. The world of marketing and advertising was not a cake walk she realized on her first day itself. She had a lot to learn and she was eager.

She left office on time as she had to go house hunting. She wanted to move to South Delhi soon so that she could avoid travelling for long hours. She sat back in her cab, relaxing her head on the car headrest, smiling as she thought of how she had met Rohit.

'God, I really want to meet him again. If we don't get the business, I will have to call and talk to him. I want to know him better.' Her heart raced as she thought of him as did the car, on the Delhi roads.

Rohit's heart was also racing, but that was because he was running on the jogging track. When he arrived home after a hectic day, he felt confused, and the only way to get out of the confusion was to run.

While on the tracks, as his foot fell on the ground, one after the other, in a rhythmic beat, his mind calmed down and he felt relaxed. He knew that after a while he would be in a state of runners' high due to the release of endorphins, hormones acting as a stimulant in the body, resulting in what many call a "natural high." He would often wonder why people who were stressed did not take up running. This should be prescribed by mental health specialists. But then, very little was being done for mental health or any health for that matter in our country. He wanted to do something to promote running as a habit in people's lives. But where was the time? There was so much he wanted to do in life, so many places he wanted to visit, so many songs that he wanted to compose and so many books that he wanted to read and write. One life was not enough! Time was too short, and he had a lot to do. So, he valued time. He did not waste time on frivolous things and certainly not on dating.

He was 27, and yet he had never been in any relationship. He was not a virgin, but then it was in college when he had indulged in casual sex with a Romanian girl who had come as an exchange student. The girl had a boyfriend back home and was not looking for love. It was his first time, and she was an expert lover. They had a torrid relationship for a few months during which time he learnt the nuances of making love. He realized that more than one's own pleasure, sex was about giving your partner a high. More than one's own orgasm, it was about making your partner quiver and moan in delight.

He was a fast learner, and his teacher, his Romanian partner, would bring the house down screaming in ecstasy when they would make love. He had to take care to close the windows and doors to muffle the screams. His biggest compliment came when she told him that he was the best lover she ever had. She left after six months. He missed her but he never tried to contact her. There were few more causal encounters but none as passionate as the one that he had with her.

He had never met any girl who had made his heart beat faster or made him want to meet her again. He liked beautiful girls, who didn't? But he always shied away from a relationship, because he had no time. He was in a hurry, in a hurry to do the things that he had always dreamt of doing.

It had been two days since he had met the two beautiful females. One was his age and seemed to be smitten by him, while the other was an older woman. He should have been responding to the girl in her twenties, but he felt drawn to the other woman. Sheetal was all that he liked in a woman. She was beautiful, poised, elegant and successful. She was very professional in her approach, and this was a refreshing change.

Many of the women he met at work would drop their professional demeanor after some time and start behaving like a woman. There was nothing wrong in that, but he felt that bringing one's femininity in professional meetings was not fair. Many females unconsciously did that, while some did it intentionally. Sheetal, he found, was unaware of his being a man. She was a thorough professional, starting with the handshake, which was tight and firm, unlike the limp handshake of most women. While making the presentation and while talking, she did not smile unnecessarily, and while discussing "sex", she did not look embarrassed or uneasy. In fact, she had looked straight into his eyes and told him that her last idea would work because sex sold like nothing else in the country.

He could see that she was desperate to close the deal, but even though he liked the idea, he wanted time to think it over. He never took any decision in a hurry, and so, once he decided something, he never regretted it. So, he had asked for more time which she had not liked.

His uncle had given his reference to Mr. Shukla, the company's owner. They had met at some international conference on spices, and when his uncle learnt that Mr. Shukla was looking for a digital marketing and advertising consultant, he had referred his name. Mr. Shukla was a man in his forties and was doing well in his field. He had started the company from scratch and now it was one of the fastest-growing companies searching for wider horizons.

Rohit had been hired with the understanding that he would take most decisions with the only condition that he would keep Mr. Shukla informed. This suited him as he did not like working with someone breathing down his neck all the time. He was clear on that.

Today, what was confusing him was his own reaction. He knew he had done the right thing by not committing anything immediately after the meeting. He needed to think but the fact that the lady was not very happy was bothering him. It should not but it did. How she had addressed him formally was not lost on him and was understandable. What was funny was why this bothered him. Why did he want to see a smile on that beautiful face? To be honest, he had picked up the phone to call her up and inform her that he was going ahead with her proposal and that the contract was hers.

He held himself back for two reasons. Firstly, he had to meet one more party before making that decision. Secondly, he wanted to see her face when he gave her the news. He wanted to see a smile break out on her face. She had a lovely smile; he had noticed that and was stunned by the way it transformed her face. He could say that she did not smile with her lips, rather with her heart. Her eyes lit up like stars and her face shone like a moon. My! My! Now he was becoming poetic! This was the effect that she had had on him and it disturbed him.

Her eyes sparkled like stars

Tresses dark as night, haloed around in style

The moon descended down on her face

Such was the beauty of her smile.

His mind thought up these lines in a jiffy, and he was startled and agitated at the same time that he had composed these lines for a female who he had met only once. Actually, he normally wrote motivational lines and poems. It had been a long time since he wrote about love and romance.

He was a rational man, and he believed that every action of ours has logic behind it. He tried to find a simple explanation for his undeniable attraction towards her. Yes, he was attracted to her there was no denying the fact. He could not remember the last time he felt drawn to a woman. To be honest, she was the first female whom he wanted to know better.

No, it was not physical attraction. Even though she was unarguably a very beautiful and desirable woman, it was more than that. He wanted to know everything about her. He wanted to know what made her tick and he wanted to know the girl behind the lovely woman that the world saw. There is always a naïve and innocent little girl hidden in every woman whatever her age, and there also is a wise and motherly woman tucked inside every little girl. He wanted to be the one to bring out the girl in her. This was too frustrating for him since he knew there was no chance. This was not because she was much older to him. That did not bother him much. He knew he would never have the opportunity to be with her because she was already married. She was Mrs. Sheetal Chopra, a much-married woman.

It was two days since they had the meeting, and he could not get her out of his mind. He would have to respond to her soon. He knew she would be waiting, but he wanted to take control of his thoughts before he spoke to her. Turning down her brilliant idea just because he was attracted to her was certainly not fair either to her or to Mr. Shukla.

'Ok. Maybe because I have been too busy working and not meeting girls my age is the reason, I feel this drawn towards an attractive woman. A married woman is a safer choice because she will never want more from a relationship. Perhaps this is why my subconscious mind is pushing me towards her.' He tried to reason with himself.

So, it would be better if he met some other girl to distract his mind away from Sheetal. A young and pretty face to his mind, eyes brimming with tears and a hassled look on her face as she picked up the papers from the floor, came to his mind.

Richa! Yes, she seemed to be interested in him. He could read her eyes. It would be good if he got to know her better. She at least, would be available and maybe then he would not think much about the other lady.

It was too late to call, but he made a mental note to call Sheetal for a meeting the next day, and he would specifically ask for Richa to also be present.

Rohit felt better after making this decision. He thought he had found a solution to his problem. Using Richa as armor, perhaps he would be protected from Sheetal's charms. Little did he know that no armor in the world was strong enough to withstand an attack when cupid decided to strike. His heart was already exposed, vulnerable and eagerly waiting for love to arrive!

The light at the traffic was about to turn red, and Sheetal applied the brake to bring her car to a screeching halt. Another car honked at the back. She looked at the rear-view mirror, and saw a young man gesturing at her to jump the red traffic light. She shook her head and switched off the ignition. The boy uttered some abuse which of course she could not hear and showed her the middle finger.

"Up yours too, you bastard," she muttered.

It was a Saturday and she was driving to the children's school. The Principal had summoned her since Saurabh's academic performance had been declining. He used to be a good student, but lately, his grades have been declining. Like always, Sanjay never found time to attend any of the PTMs. It was her responsibility. So today she was going to the school to get a lecture about how she was failing as a parent.

Sheetal was not in the best of her moods. Normally a happy go lucky person she often found herself feeling low these days. Lately, she had never been able to give time to herself. It had been ages since she had written anything. It had been months since she had read a good book.

Listening to Mehdi Hassan's ghazals at night with lights dimmed and a glass of wine in her hand used to be her idea of bliss. The soothing melodious voice would often soothe her heart and relax her mind so much that she would fall asleep. These days she was either so tired that she would go off to sleep the moment she hit the bed or lay awake thinking about something that had happened at the office or about something that Sanjay had said or done to annoy her. Most days, it was Sanjay's snoring that would put her to sleep.

Sanjay was another of her problems. Life's irony was that when you had something, you didn't want it and when you didn't have the same thing you would wonder why. In the initial years of their marriage, they would make love every night. She enjoyed it. After a few years, it came down to twice or thrice a week. Since the last few years, it had come down to once a month and only when Sanjay would demand it. She would be too tired to respond and all she would want was to sleep. Sanjay complained that she was cold and frigid.

She tried to explain to him that managing two growing boys and two adult men was no easy task; It seeped out all energy but he did not understand and often blamed her for their dwindling sex life. Even though she flinched inwardly every time he called her an "ice maiden", she tried not to show.

It was lately that she got concerned because in the last six months, they had not made love even once. What was more worrying was that he had also stopped taunting her about her lack of interest and even though she had tried to initiate sex a couple of times, he had turned her down. Initially, she thought he was trying to get even by refusing, but lately her intuition was telling her something was wrong. You may call it womanly instinct, but whatever it was, she felt that there was another woman in his life.

Whenever she thought about this being a possibility, she would feel a funny vacuum in her heart. She wanted him to make love to her, but he did not. She wanted him to show by his actions that he cared for her, but he did not. She wanted to ask him about it, but the mere thought of bringing up the subject made her feel humiliated and degraded.

She wanted to discuss this with someone, but with who? She did not have many friends, one of the many prices a working woman pays for she does not have time to nurture too many relationships. Even the few friends that she had were wives of Sanjay's friends. She could not discuss this with anyone, not even her best friend. How could she? Neither could she berate her husband in front of anyone nor did she want anyone in the world to pity her.

Moreover, her best friend, stayed in the US and would not understand the situation. She would give some outrageous advice, and they would end up arguing. So, she did not know what to do and who to discuss this with. Her mother, had she been alive today, perhaps would have advised her, but she had passed away a year back. She felt utterly and desperately lonely.

Office was another of her concerns. She needed the job, and for that she needed new orders. There were not many in the pipeline. Following the Lalwani incident, many good clients, who she should have handled, were passed to her male counterparts. She desperately needed the SAC spices account. Damn that boy! Rohit was his name. He was taking too much time to arrive at a decision. That was the problem with the young generation. They were inconsistent. In certain things, they would be in a tearing hurry, and in others, they would behave as if they had all the time in the world. Time was running out for her. At work, the constant barbs from Dracula were getting on her nerves while Sanjay was making things difficult at home.

It was just then that her phone rang. She glanced at it and a smile broke out on her face. It was that boy calling! But then a sense of nervousness engulfed her. What if he called to inform her that they had decided not to give them the business?

'Come-on Sheetal, be positive and smile. The positivity will take you another mile!' She rhymed and took the call.

"Good morning Mrs. Chopra," Rohit said. "I am sorry for the delay, but I was wondering if we could meet today to close the deal."

Sheetal felt a huge sense of relief wash over her.

'Thank God! Thank God!' She would have to remember to go to the temple and offer *Prasad* for Rs 501 which had been her prior arrangement with God.

"Oh! Certainly. What time will be convenient?" She asked. "And thank you Mr. Jain for placing your trust on us. I assure you that we will not let you down."

"I am sure it will be a pleasure working with your team Mrs. Chopra," he said.

This was the second time he had addressed her as Mrs. Chopra. She remembered having told him to call her Sheetal. Did she look so old that he had to "Mrs. Chopra" her. 'Well, two could play at a game,' she thought.

"It will be a pleasure for us too Mr. Jain," she replied.

"What time are we meeting?" She repeated.

"Can we have lunch together? Say at one?" Rohit replied.

"Oh! I am so sorry Mr. Jain. I am on the way to my son's school right now. He is going to appear for the 12th Board exams next year. His grades are slipping so, I have been summoned to the school for a lecture. Can we make it at 2?" She asked, trying to laugh off her nervousness.

She could not take the risk of him cancelling the meeting. She needed to close this deal at the earliest, but at the same time, this school meeting was also important.

"No issues, Mrs. Chopra. We will meet at two. Please come to Café Tesu near the petrol pump at the IIT gate, and please bring your team along," Rohit said.

"Team?" Sheetal was confused for a moment.

"The intern, what was her name…mmm Richa?"

"Oh Ok. I will have to ask her to come. Though it will be a short notice for her," she replied. "Today, being Saturday, she must be having her own plans, but don't worry, I will ask her to be there," she said immediately.

There was no way she was going to goof this up. 'If I have to drag the girl to the meeting I will do it,' she thought to herself.

"I appreciate it. It will help if we all are on the same platform from the beginning. Anyway, she will be involved in the day-to-day working so, she better be involved in the project right from day one," Rohit said.

'Well, well, this is a bit too much,' she thought, not liking the way he was trying to impose his idea on her. It was their prerogative to decide who would work on the project. But she didn't say anything and just agreed to meet him at Essex farms along with Richa.

'That boy seems to be smitten by Richa. Ah, to be young again,' she thought.

At her age, anyone who showed interest in her had only one thing on their mind, and in which she was not interested.

When was the last time that she had gone for coffee or drinks with a man other than her husband? She couldn't remember, but whenever it was, it was either for work or with some old friend. It was nothing like a date.

Sheetal was a romantic at heart. 'A handsome man to dine, with roses and wine' was her thing. Well! To be honest, being handsome wasn't any criteria. A man who was sensitive, witty, caring and creative was her type of man. 'Alas! They don't make such men anymore,' she thought.

Did they ever? She smiled wryly as she reached for her phone to call Richa.

Richa could not believe she had heard right when Sheetal called her and asked her to reach Essex Farm at 2. She did not enquire if Richa was free but just gave the instructions to be there. Richa had been checking out a few flats along with her property agent, when Sheetal had called, and she had to rush to her home to change.

She was meeting him again! Thank God! She was casually dressed in shorts and a tee-shirt and so, could not go for the meeting directly before changing. She would have to rush to her flat and then go to Essex Farm. God! There wasn't that much time!

She was in Greater Kailash and going to West Delhi and then returning to IIT Gate wasn't possible in such a short time.

'I have no option but to buy something and change into it,' she thought. So, she decided to go the FAB India store and pick up something to wear.

Never had she ever shopped in such a tearing hurry, but when she saw the result in the shop's dressing room, she was happy with her decision to shop and change. She had chosen a light pink Kota cotton kurta with white lace at the sleeves with the hem accentuating her soft frame. She paired this with white trousers. Indo-western dressing was always a safe bet. Whether ethnic or formal, one could never look overdressed or underdressed. She liked what saw in the mirror, but something was lacking. Yes, she needed to change her earrings!

She went to the jewelry section and looked around. A pair of polka earrings in white was slightly bigger than what she normally wore, but it would go with her ensemble perfectly. She bought the earrings. Like most women, she carried her world in her bag. She did find a light pink lipstick and mascara in her bag and used her lipstick as a blusher and shadow. This was a hack she had learnt lately. After all her efforts, the result was eye-catching to say the least. She looked beautiful and she knew it. She applied some perfume to her wrist and was ready to go.

Dressing up always gave her a high, and today, since she had dressed up for a special person, she felt a nervous excitement.

She called a cab to take her to the café. It was a nice place just by the side of a petrol pump. Luckily, she reached there before time.

It was a small turquoise building with vibrant rustic colour and large windows. The interior was well-lit and looked inviting. The café was quite spacious and had a small library in a corner, some modern back lights, a live coffee and dessert display counter, some vibrant graffiti on a few walls and vintage, wooden tables and chairs.

She chose a table for three that over-looked the busy main road as it gave an eerie sense of calm amidst the bustling chaos of an urban setup.

She glanced at her phone. It was ten minutes to two. She texted Sheetal informing her that she had arrived and sat back in her chair watching the chaos outside. Which one was more chaotic, the road or her thoughts? She smiled at her own thought and took a few deep breaths to calm her heart which was beating so loud that she felt people on the next table could hear her heartbeats! She took a sip of water to calm her and glanced at the restaurant's glass door.

A car pulled up in the roadside parking which was visible from where she was sitting and a lady got out of it. It took her a few seconds to realize that the lady was her boss, Sheetal. She was wearing a blue denim jean and a white tee-shirt. A fancy sunglass was perched up her nose. Her hair was tied in a ponytail, and she looked very different from what she looked like at work. Actually, she looked young and smart. Had she dressed up to impress Rohit? A tiny doubt nagged at the back of her mind, but then she laughed at her stupidity. Firstly, she was much older to Rohit. Perhaps, biologically old enough to be his mother and secondly, unlike her, she was casually dressed and not dressed up.

Richa waved at her to catch her eye. "Ma'am," she called out. Sheetal noticed her and came to where she was sitting.

Richa got up to greet her. They shook hands and Sheetal said, "I like to be addressed by my first name. Call me Sheetal. Ma'am makes me feel old and ancient."

"Sure Ma'am, err Sheetal," Richa replied, and they laughed.

"Oh! You look very beautiful. That Is a very pretty kurta. FabIndia?" She asked.

"Thanks. Yes, Fabindia," she smiled back.

"Looks like you were dressed up to go out. Sorry I had to drag you here, but Rohit insisted that you should also come so that all of us are in sync." Sheetal told her not sounding apologetic at all.

Richa's heart missed a beat. 'Had he insisted that she should be present also? Wow! This meant he wanted to see her again! Did he feel the same attraction towards her as she felt drawn towards him?'

"Rohit called me. He is reaching in ten minutes. Let's order something while we wait for him." Sheetal gestured towards the waiter for the menu.

"They serve lovely Sushi here and the pastries are awesome," she said as she looked at the menu.

They ordered a platter of Sushi and some sandwiches. Sheetal ordered a large latte for herself while Richa ordered a black coffee.

There was an awkward silence as they waited for their food and Rohit.

"Where are your parents?" Sheetal broke the silence.

"They are in Haldia. My father works for Hindustan Levers," she replied with a smile. It was good that she was asking personal questions. They had hardly had any personal conversation till now.

"I am looking for a place in south Delhi." She offered the information.

"Yes. You should. It's always better to stay near the workplace. I stay in Greater Kailash-1 which is near our office. My children's school is also near where we reside. In fact, I am coming from there after attending the PTM."

"How old are your children?" Richa asked.

"My elder son is 16 and the younger one is 14," Sheetal replied. A soft smile played on her face when the spoke.

"Well, you don't look as if you have grown up children," remarked Richa.

"Well thanks. I don't have my legs in the grave though." Sheetal laughed and looked up to see Rohit standing there. They had failed to notice him enter the restaurant.

They exchanged greetings as he pulled a chair next to Richa at the four-seater table. Suddenly, Richa was conscious of his presence. She turned her chair towards left so she could see him, not his profile.

They ordered some more sandwiches and a cappuccino for him.

He looked at Sheetal and said, "I want to congratulate both of you for the excellent presentation. We have decided to give the contract to you. The formal work order will be sent, but before doing that, I wanted to be sure that we are clear on our expectations."

Sheetal nodded as he continued.

"As I have already conveyed to you Mrs. Chopra, I want you to coordinate the day-to-day work. Of course, we will have meetings with your and my bosses whenever any important decision has to be taken." He turned towards Richa as he spoke.

Her heart skipped another beat. She nodded.

"If you don't mind, I have a request. Please drop this Mrs. Chopra business and call me Sheetal." She smiled at Rohit.

"Sure, Sheetal," Rohit said her name slowly as if savoring it.

They sat and continued the discussion as they had their food. After it was over, Sheetal called for the bill. Rohit insisted on paying, but Sheetal would have none of it.

"I am much senior to both of you, and moreover, it's on the company's account," she said firmly.

They went out together. Rohit insisted that Sheetal should depart first. Richa had to wait for a cab, and he insisted that he would leave only after seeing her off.

"What a chivalrous man!" She thought as they waved back at Sheetal, who drove out of place waving to them.

They waited for her cab to arrive.

"Was she upset that I took time to decide?" He asked.

She was taken aback by the question and did not know what to say. She decided to be honest.

"Though she did not say anything directly, but I think she was upset," she replied, looking straight at him.

There was a faraway look on his face as if he was not there with her.

Just then the cab arrived and she got inside. He closed the door for her and smiled at her.

"Take care," he said. "We will be meeting soon." This time their eyes met, and she felt her heart skip a beat as the car went out of the gate.

Sheetal was happy when she reached home. She wanted to share the news with someone, but there was no one there other than Mr. Subramanian who would be happy with the news. He was delighted when she gave him the news that they had got the business. He also praised her, which off-late, was becoming rare.

The boys were out playing, and she went to the kitchen to prepare dinner. She did not feel like cooking. It had been long since they had gone out together as a family. Sanjay never had time these days. His company had five working days, but he always went to his office even on Saturdays. Previously, he would go but only during quarter closing. Lately he was going every Saturday.

She called him up, and after a while, he picked up the phone.

"Can we have dinner out today?" She asked.

"You don't feel like cooking again, is it?" His words tore into her heart, and for a moment, she wanted to retort with a nasty comment, but she managed to control her temper.

"No, it's not that. I got a major business deal today and thought we could celebrate."

He mellowed down. "I am having a team meeting now, followed by dinner. I will not be able to join. You go ahead with the boys."

'Team meeting on a Saturday?' Sheetal wondered. The feeling that something was wrong had been gnawing at her for long. She did not want to go deep into it. When you know that the path is dark and murky, you tend to avoid it. But for how long could she ignore her feelings?

She needed to do something to find out what was happening. She had a strong feeling that someone else was in his life. He would not leave his phone even for a minute nowadays. Sometimes he would go out of the room with his phone and speak in hushed tones. Sometimes, at night, when he thought she was sleeping, he would type on his phone.

She went to bed and lay down, closing her eyes and thinking about what she could do. All the euphoria of bagging the contract vanished into thin air. After a while, she got up with a determined look. She would do what she had never done, snoop around.

She checked his wardrobe. In between the papers, she found a bill from Tanishq. It was for a pendant set costing 1.25 lacs. He had never given her any pendant set! For whom had he bought this set? There were some restaurant bills also. If these were official meetings, he should have claimed them from his office. Why were they here?

Sheetal reached for her phone and looked for a number. Kunal was a Deputy General Manager in Sanjay's team. She liked him, and she knew that the feeling was mutual. His wife also clicked with her whenever they met at official parties. They had invited them to their house once, and she remembered having a nice time.

"Kunal, can I speak to Sanjay. I have been unable to reach his number." She lied.

"He is not with me. I am at home," he replied.

"Are you not in the team meeting?" She asked.

"What meeting? We did not go to the office today as we are having pest control in the building," he said, and then, they both realized what it meant.

"Oh! I am sorry," she replied quickly. "I might have got it wrong." She hung up.

The sinking feeling in her heart was real. It was so real that it felt as if she was going down. Truth, when it hits you, it hurts.

She still wanted to give him another chance. She called Sanjay again.

"Please, Sanjay. Can you not make it for dinner today?" She pleaded.

"Sheetal, I have already told you we are having a team meeting in the office. I had to come out to talk to you." He sounded irritated.

She quietly hung up, and it was then that tears started to roll down her cheeks.

Even after confirming to Sheetal that the contract was awarded to them, Rohit did not call her up for the next few days He wanted some time to deal with his feelings. He knew it was important that he did not meet her very often as proximity would only add fuel to the fire already burning in his heart. He did not believe in love, never had. This feeling was something very new to him. He wanted to learn to cope with it before he met her again. He had hoped that she would call up but she did not. He was surprised as she had shown interest in starting the work immediately, and so it was strange that there was no phone call from her.

On Wednesday, he got a call. It was not from Sheetal but from Richa. She informed him that Sheetal was sick and was on leave. Hearing this, he wanted to go and meet her and see how she was. This was absurd. How could he? He had just met her and that too officially. He was surprised at his own reaction. What was that funny feeling, that nagging worry in his head? Was it a concern for her? Why?

He had no answers. He thought for a while and called her up. She did not take the call. Later, in the evening, she called back.

Her voice sounded like a child's on the phone, sweet and innocent. Listening to her, it was obvious that she was not well. The authority, the confidence and the gaiety were missing from her voice.

"Didn't Richa tell you that I am not well?" She asked.

"Yes, she did. I wanted to know if you are better now," he replied and then added "Mrs. Chopra" as an afterthought.

This time she did not tell him to address her as Sheetal.

"I am better. I will be joining office next week maybe. I have told my boss to handover this assignment to someone else if you want it to be completed soon."

'No,' he thought. 'No, no, I don't want that. I want you.' He wanted to say but remained speechless.

"We will see. You get well soon," he said as he disconnected the call.

It was a week since that fateful day when she had come to terms with the fact that her marriage was on the rocks. She had hired a detective and found out, in just a few days, that Sanjay was having an affair with Riya. Riya was a manager in Sanjay's team. She was in her early thirties and a divorcee. She lived near their house, so she would come to pick him up when Sanjay's car would go for servicing. He also gave her lifts often. She was simple-looking but attractive and maintained herself well.

Sheetal did not do anything with the proof that the detective had collected. She did not want to rock the marriage boat yet. She had to first be sure of what she wanted for herself. What if he wanted a divorce? Would she want one too? She decided to let it remain buried in her heart till the time that either he confessed himself or she would know for sure what she wanted.

She had been thinking about what had gone wrong. In spite of Sanjay's nature and behavior, she had tried her best to adjust.

She had really tried hard and accepted him as he was. Perhaps she had not been as demonstrative and affectionate wife as she should have been, but neither was he. Moreover, managing a household with four males and a demanding job was never easy.

She blamed herself for not taking any corrective measures even when she felt he was withdrawing from her, but what could she do? How can you force someone to love you if they have fallen out of love? Had he ever loved her or had he just been tolerating her?

Even though she was a romantic and believed in love, in her own case, she felt that she had failed miserably. They were two strangers married to each other by their parents and forced by society to stay together and raise a family, when in fact, they were just not suited for each other. She, being a woman, had compromised and accepted this as her fate, but he had found someone else in his life to make his life worth living. Could she really blame him?

Had she not been tempted to respond to a colleague who had shown interest in her some five years ago? It could easily have turned into an affair, but she had controlled herself. Why had she? She would have loved being wooed, being taken to dinners, being gifted precious gifts and also made sensuous love to.

She had not succumbed to desire but he had! She was not angry anymore at Sanjay but she was sad, very sad. She felt utterly alone and the fear that he would ask for a divorce was eroding her from inside. She did not want to be divorced, she realized after introspection. She wanted her marriage intact not only for the boys but also for own selfish reasons.

Being married gave her a sense of security. It gave her a home filled with some semblance of sanity in the chaotic world. Sheetal's mother was no more, and her father lived with her brother in Auckland. The only home she had and the only place she could call her home was this place. She had nowhere to go. She did not want to go. She would have to close her eyes to what was happening right under her nose. She would have to suppress the voice that sometimes asked her to fight for self-respect. She would have to become an ostrich and act as if there was no storm in her life only because she refused to acknowledge it.

She pretended to be sick to avoid going to office. She needed time to digest this. She did not have to pretend because she actually felt sick. She felt like she was already dead. There were bouts of depression when she would cry, but she was careful not to do it in front of the boys and Sanjay. Sanjay was considerate. He made her talk to their family doctor over the phone and got the medicines. He also got fruits and juice for her. The boys were also caring and were on their prefect behavior. If she could just block the proof from her mind, she could pretend that everything was fine.

She joined office on Monday after a week's leave. Dracula was kind and offered to give her lighter assignment if she wanted.

No, she wanted to scream at him. She wanted to immerse herself in the work. She called for a meeting of her team and took stock of all the old projects that were running. Then she enquired about the SAC spices case. It had not started yet as the client had preferred to wait for her to join. She remembered that Rohit had wanted Richa to be involved, so she asked her to call him up and fix a meeting.

She worked throughout the day, and when she looked at the watch, it was already seven. She packed her stuff and was about to leave when Richa walked in.

"Ma'am, the meeting with Rohit has been fixed for 10 am tomorrow at his office. Is it fine with you?" She asked.

"Yes," Sheetal replied.

"Am I required there?" Richa asked.

"Of course! I have told you to be involved in the project, haven't I? So why ask this question?" She almost shouted at her and immediately regretted it. She was venting out her frustrations on the poor girl.

"*Sorry Ma'am. I will be there.*" Richa's face fell, as she left the room quickly.

The moment that Richa was out of the room she burst into tears. It was a simple enough question that Richa had asked, and Sheetal need not have shouted at her. Just then her phone rang. It was Rohit's call. He probably wanted to ask her if the meeting was confirmed.

Richa wiped away her tears and said, "hello". She must have sounded funny, because he immediately asked her if anything was wrong. She lost control over herself as tears rolled down her cheeks once again. He let her sob on the phone for some time and then asked her where she was.

"I was about to leave the office," she replied trying to control her tears.

"Meet me in the Rose café in GK-2 market in twenty minutes," he told her not even wanting to know if she had something else lined up.

'Even if I had, I would have cancelled it,' she thought even as she agreed to meet him.

In less than thirty minutes both of them were sitting in Rose Café. This was the first time that they were meeting unofficially. It could be called their first date. There would be many in the days to come, of that, she was sure.

She ordered a cappuccino while he asked for a frappe.

Even though she wasn't felling hungry, he insisted that they order a chocolate muffin for her.

"It's a happy food, and it will do wonders for your mood," he said.

'He is so sensitive and caring,' she thought once again. *'He takes control of the situation and allows others to lean on him.' It would be so nice to have someone like him in her life.*

"Now tell me what is bothering you," he asked as a matter of fact. "You should be smiling and enjoying life, not sobbing."

Richa found herself narrating the incident that had taken place.

Rohit looked surprised. It was difficult to imagine Sheetal shouting at anyone. What was wrong with her?

"It may be her illness. She has returned from being sick in bed. She may not be feeling all that good." He tried to justify her action.

"Yes, that is what I think too," she said, disliking that he was supporting Sheetal. They sat talking to each other for nearly two hours.

Both of them found the other very easy to converse with. Once the conversation started about work Sheetal was forgotten. Soon Richa found herself laughing at his jokes.

'I can easily fall in love with him,' she thought as she sipped her third cup of coffee. She did not want to leave. She wanted this moment to go on forever.

It was Rohit who pointed at the watch and said that they should be leaving. He offered to drop her at her place. It was only the previous week that she had shifted to her new flat in Saket, which was not very far, so she accepted his offer.

As he dropped her at her flat, she asked him if he wanted to come in for another cup of coffee.

He looked into her eyes and smiled. "I will surely take up that offer some other time," he said as he accelerated the car and zoomed away into the night.

The moment he saw her the next day, he knew something was wrong. No one could change so much in just a week. Rohit could not believe she was the same Sheetal he had met only a few days ago.

She looked like the epitome of grief. Her eyes were dead and lifeless and would suddenly go vacant amid their conversation. She looked very distracted and lost, as if her heart was not in the meeting and the discussions they were having.

Just a few days of fever could not bring about such a personality change. Something had happened to her Rohit was sure but did not know how to ask her.

Sheetal was very nice to Richa, perhaps trying to make up for her unjustified anger the previous evening. Richa was slightly cold towards her, not wanting to forgive so easily. He was like a spectator, looking and trying to decipher the play of human emotions.

None of them mentioned about their meeting the previous day. It remained their secret. They had met on a personal level. It had nothing to do with work anyway.

Their meeting continued till evening, and they had lunch in his office. The undercurrent of the morning was sorted, and by the end of the day, Richa was behaving normally with Sheetal.

Sheetal was also looking better, but even then, Rohit knew in his heart that something was constantly on Sheetal's mind that was unrelated to work in any way.

Earlier, she was a confident, elegant and beautiful woman, but now poignant and mysterious were two adjectives that he could add. All these were making her too enticing, and he knew that he wanted to know her better and become close to her.

He wanted her to open up with him and share with him whatever was bothering her. He knew it was a pipe dream. There was no way she would do that. He was just a client to her and nothing more. She had no idea that what he felt for her was nothing to do with a client and vendor relationship. He did not know what he felt, but he knew that whatever it was, it was sweet yet scary. It was drawing her to him like a magnet, and yet he knew he could never have her. Looking at her smiling was so beautiful, yet the pain in her eyes made him feel heavy in his heart. Was this alien feeling love? He brushed aside the thought.

His evening, the day before, with Richa had been very good. After a long time, he had been with a female without any intention of having sex. He had enjoyed her company and had felt happy that he could make her laugh with his jokes. They had not realized how time had passed and that they had been in the café for more than two hours.

When she had invited him to her flat, he knew what she was offering. It was clearly visible on her face. She was attracted to him, he could tell. Perhaps he too was, but he was not sure.

Could a person be attracted to two people at the same time?

'No, what I feel for Sheetal is much more than mere attraction. It can be called an obsession if not love,' he told himself.

'I have to do something about it. I cannot hanker after a much older and married woman.' He would not have bothered about the age difference had she been single. He would have proposed to her if she was a divorcee, even with a child. But she was not. She had a family – a husband and two boys. Maybe she also had a dog and a balcony in her house where she would sip tea with her husband. Maybe she had a table where all four family members would talk during dinner time, a house that reverberated with laughter and a master-bed where she moaned in ecstasy while her husband made love to her.

'No, I cannot think of her. I have to stop,' he thought for the nth time.

"Richa, where do you stay?" He asked, pretending in the presence of Sheetal that he did not know.

"Saket," she replied with a smile, playing along with him.

"Come, I will drop you," he said. "I am going that way."

With great difficulty Richa maintained a straight face as she mumbled her thanks.

The three left the office together - one with a gloomy heart, the other with her heart racing like a formula 1 racing car and the third with a heart so confused that he did not know what it wanted.

Sheetal was sitting at her desk, fiddling with her pen and staring into space. These days she was merely pulling on trying to block her thought process. Human emotions are so complex. The more you want to brush away certain thoughts or feelings, the more they cling to you.

The more that Sheetal tried to brush the fact that her husband was having an affair, under the carpet the more it would come back to haunt her. Every action that Sanjay did now was treated with suspicion.

Every evening that he would be late, every night that he would say that he had a "business dinner", every time that he did not take her call, she told herself that he was with 'her'.

Every time he opened his mouth to say something to her, she feared that he would confess to her about his affair and ask her for a divorce.

She had been to a circus as a child and seen women walking on a rope. She would wonder if they did not fear falling down. They could slip and fall any moment. How did they feel?

She knew the feeling now. She felt like an acrobat, and she knew she could come crashing down at any moment. Her world would crumble in front of her eyes.

It was now nearly three months that she had been living with the dreadful knowledge about her husband in her heart. The pain had subsided considerably by now, but the fear would not leave her. She could not imagine a life without her family. Sanjay was a good husband and a good father. In spite of his nagging and his barbs, he provided the support she needed badly. She sometimes thought she was a parasite taking energy from her family. If she was not there, perhaps they would manage with a domestic help, but without them in her life, she would not be able to live, let alone be happy.

Work was progressing at a slow pace. Her heart was not in her work, and she knew it. Even then, her work was the only solace in her life. The only time that she did not fear that Sanjay would ask for a divorce was when she was working!

Even during this time, when her mind was in chaos, much to her surprise, she had noticed something very strange. Rohit would often look at her intensely which conveyed a lot to her. But the moment she looked at him, he would turn his face away. In the beginning, when she had noticed him looking at her, she thought that it was her imagination but later, she was sure.

He was infatuated with her. Perhaps he desired her. A woman can never go wrong with her gut feeling. Rohit certainly saw her as a desirable woman though he was careful enough never to cross the line.

She was reminded of the time in office when Devesh, one of her team members, had proposed to her. They had been working on a project that required working late hours and travelling out-station. They had become friendlier than she had ever been with her colleagues. She enjoyed the attention that Devesh would give her as a boss and a woman. He never forgot to compliment her and would notice everything about her. Even a new ear-ring that she would wear would not go unnoticed. He would compliment her on her choice, her taste in clothes, and her beauty.

She enjoyed the attention and the compliments that he showered on her. She was after all a woman, and which woman would not melt when compliments are given sincerely?

He had once asked her if she had a sister because he wanted to marry someone like her. She had blushed and had not reprimanded him for saying such a thing. On her birthday, he had got a gift for her, a beautiful red saree. It was too personal a gift to be accepted from a male colleague, but she had taken it.

One day he told her that he loved her. *"I know you are married so I can't propose marriage, but can we remain friends, maybe a little more than friends? There is no harm in stealing some moments for ourselves in this world where everyone is busy running a race."*

She knew what he meant. She was tempted to say "yes" and bask in the glory of being loved again. She wanted to feel the romance, the quickened heartbeats and that phase when everything in life seemed like a fairy tale once again.

But she could not. She was married. She could not let herself get carried away with her emotions. So, she said "No" when her heart wanted to say "yes".

Devesh put in his papers the next day and was gone. Before leaving, he met her to bid goodbye.

"I know what I proposed to you was wrong in the eyes of society. But if God considered it to be wrong, he would not have made anyone fall in love with any married person. Love does not get bound by man-made rules. You are not the first woman I loved and you will not be the last, but I can say with all honesty that I truly and genuinely love you. Being so close to you and yet maintaining the distance would be very difficult for me. So, I am quitting the job. Hoping that one day I will be able to remember you with pure love and not love laced with pain. If ever you need me, I will be there." He kissed her hands and walked out of the room. There were tears in his eyes and her eyes were moist too.

She missed him terribly and wanted to message him, talk to him, but she did not. She was strong. She was a mother. She was a wife. She had controlled her emotions then.

Even now, at her age, she found that young men would show interest in her. She could take it further and have a good time if she wanted. For instance, if she wanted, she just had to show some interest in Rohit and they could be having an affair. But she did not want an affair. She wanted her husband to love her. If that was too much to ask for then she would settle for her husband just showing some interest in her. This too was missing, and now the affair!

Sheetal was lost in her thoughts when her phone rang. She went numb when she saw the name that flashed on her phone. It was Riya calling. What she dreaded was going to happen.

'Sanjay did not dare to come out in open so he was taking the help of his girlfriend', she thought.

With a sinking heart, she took the call.

"Sheetal, this is Riya."

There was silence and neither of them spoke.

"I think you know why I am calling."

"No, I don't." Sheetal found herself speaking.

'Why should I make it easy for her?' She thought.

"Well, I think you know. Even if you don't, I want to tell you that Sanjay and I are in love with each other. It's only the thought of the boys that is keeping him in a relation when there is nothing else to hold him."

'Nothing? What about all the years of her life that she had sacrificed looking after him and his family? What about the months that she had nursed him when he had broken his leg? What about the nights when she had stayed awake caring for him when he was sick or the hours she had waited for him to return home at night so she could serve him hot food? None of the reasons were strong enough to hold him?' She had wanted to ask, but she kept quiet.

"I think we should meet to discuss this. It is better that Sanjay does not know about it. We women should first talk about it and try to sort it out."

'Sort it out? As if they were two girls playing doll house and deciding who would have the doll,' she thought. This suddenly felt funny and she started laughing.

Riya was perhaps not prepared for such reaction, and she hung up the phone, mumbling something inaudible.

Sheetal found herself laughing uncontrollably and slowly the laughter turned into sobs. The dam burst. Her control over her emotions broke, and she found herself sobbing, oblivious to her surroundings.

Rohit knocked on the door, but there was no response. He could hear Sheetal laughing and he knocked again, a little loudly this time. The door was open so he hesitatingly pushed it a bit more. That was when he saw her sobbing with her head on the table.

He did not know what to do. They had a meeting at three. He had come a little early and thought of having tea with her before talking shop.

After spending the previous three months with her, he was very sure that she was his kind of a woman- warm, witty, wise and having a way with words. During their conversations they had found out they had many things in common. Of all things, they both loved to rhyme sentences! They would often talk in verses having an *antakshri* of their own kind. It would go on and on and none would give up. Richa often acted as judge and would declare a winner. She would always choose her boss, and Rohit would pretend to be offended.

The three of them had come close and got along well. But all along there was something that Sheetal was trying to hide, some hurt or pain that she was trying to cloak with her fake smiles and her laughter.

Looking at her crying her heart out, he knew he was right. She was going through some dark phase in her life all alone. His first instinct was to take her in his arms and ask her what was troubling her, but he checked himself. He took the jug from the table and poured a glass of water. Sheetal looked up and immediately realized that it was too late. He had seen her crying, and it was no use pretending otherwise. She drank the water he had poured for her and took the tissues that he handed her. She tried to control her sobbing. Rohit held her by her elbow and steered her out of the room. She did not protest. She wanted to run away to some place where she could lose herself.

Rohit did not know where he would be taking her. He just opened the car door and helped her sit on the passenger seat. He then drove out of the building. He drove the car through the traffic. They did not talk. She was quiet as he drove to Lodhi garden. He gently helped her out of the car and guided her to a nearby bench. The park was empty at this time of the day. This was why he had gone there. She, with her tears, would have attracted attention in a restaurant.

Sitting on the bench, he turned towards her and reached for her hand. He held her hand as if giving her his strength.

"Do you want to talk about it?" This was the first sentence that he uttered.

Instead of replying, she turned towards him, put her arms around him, and broke down again. She sobbed in his arms as he held her lightly, stroking her head gently. She cried for some time and then drew apart. She told him the entire story as if he were some dear friend. She needed to talk about this with someone. She needed to spew the venom she had been hiding in her heart for a long time. She spoke about sacrificing her life for her husband and his family. She spoke about how her career, in spite of being equally qualified as her husband, always took a secondary seat. She had got offers to take up projects in foreign countries, but she always had to decline because her family could not do without her. Suddenly, no one needed her now! She spoke about her compromises in life and how she was never good enough for her husband. Her husband's girlfriend wanting her to free him was the last straw.

He sat there listening to her pour out her anguish and her pain.

"Did you eat anything?" He asked. "Come, let's grab something to eat", he said and drove to a near by restaurant. She was composed now. Tears clear the vision as they wash away the confusion in mind.

"I have to go. It's late. My boys would be alone", she said

"Before confronting him be sure of what you want", he said.

Did she know what she wanted? She was not sure anymore. Rohit dropped her at her house. Sanjay had not come home, and the boys were studying. She went to her room and lay down. His words rang in her ears repeatedly, making her feel unwanted and worthless with every passing second. 'No, she would not stay if she was not wanted, but it would also not be at the lady's behest that she would leave. Let Sanjay ask her to leave. Why had he sent his girlfriend to do the dirty job? He should have had the guts to face her.'

'Rohit was right', she thought. *'I will pretend as if nothing has happened. Let him start the topic.'* She bought herself some more time of dignified existence before the dirt was out in the open.

The boys came searching for her and, seeing her in her room, thought she was unwell. Sheetal told them to serve themselves food from the kitchen.

'They should get used to doing things themselves. Their new mother will not pamper them the way I used to.' She thought. This thought brought another bout of tears.

She could hear Sanjay coming into the bedroom. The boys must have told him that she was not well as he did not wake her up. Perhaps Riya had already warned him that the cat was out of the bag!

After a while she could hear him get into the bed beside her. No one spoke. They were like two strangers who had walked together for a while only to find out their paths were different. The love, the intimacy and the togetherness, were all so momentary. They exist solely in the moment only to fizzle out like a bursting bubble.

Lately, Sanjay's behavior had undergone a drastic change. He was not his usual complaining and bitchy self. He was quieter and adjusting. If there was no towel in the bathroom, he would get it himself. If the bed was not spic and span, he would not shout. He would eat whatever was before him without making faces and complaining. The children, who had no idea of what was brewing, were surprised. That morning Shashank came to her and asked, "Ma, if you don't mind my asking, why can't papa always be like this? Whatever it is that you are doing to make him happy, can't you always do it?" He asked in all his innocence, unaware of the storm brewing on the horizon.

Sheetal knew the reason why his behavior had changed. This had nothing to do with what she was doing right, rather it had everything to do with what he was doing wrong. It was possible that Riya would have told him that she had spoken to Sheetal. It could also be that Sheetal's cold behavior and pained expressions had given the game away. Whatever it was, she was sure that he had an inkling that Sheetal already knew about him and Riya.

They both were now playing a game of wait and watch. Both were cold but polite, speaking to each other only when necessary. Both were avoiding bringing up a topic which they were unsure of where it would take them.

That night after finishing her household work Sheetal went to her bedroom. Normally by now, Sanjay would be already sleeping. To her surprise, he was awake and appeared to be waiting for her.

Sheetal's sixth sense told her that he was waiting for her to talk about it today. She panicked. She was in no position to take his admission of guilt of his extramarital affair. She was tired and had no strength left for an emotional breakdown. She wanted to slip under the covers of her bed and go into a sleep so deep from which no one could wake her up. She wanted to put the clock back when all had been well. Maybe her married life hadn't been that great in the past, but it had been stable. One gets used to the idiosyncrasies of a person over time. She was now used to Sanjay's eccentricities and knew how to handle them. What she was not used to was his indifference. All her life nothing in this household could be moved in her absence. If she would be out of house for a few hours and Sanjay would be at home, there would be at least a couple of calls asking her something or the other. The person who could not go a single day without her had suddenly stopped needing her altogether? Was it sudden or was it gradual? Was Riya too beautiful to resist or had Sheetal become too repulsive? What had changed? Why had this happened? She had many questions, but she never wanted to ask them.

Sheetal looked away from Sanjay and slipped inside the covers on her side of the bed. She closed her eyes and wished for sleep to take her into oblivion.

"Sheetal, we need to talk," Sanjay said.

Sheetal felt as if her heart missed many beats. She wanted to say something but no words came out of her mouth. 'So that moment has come.' That moment that she had been dreading had arrived! All pretense of normalcy would be over. The dirt and the muck would be out. She feared mudslinging and calling names but most of all, she feared her own self. She did not want to sound pathetic, and she did not want to grovel. What if she lost control of her emotions and pleaded with him not to leave her?

"I know you are not sleeping," Sanjay said as he nudged her from behind. "Sheetal, it is very important that we talk now."

Sheetal was jolted to the present as she came back to reality. Praying to Sai Baba to give her strength, she turned towards him and opened her eyes. He was sitting with his pillow propped behind him on the bed rest. She too sat down on her side of the bed and kept the pillow on her lap to hide her clenched fingers.

She would not make it easy for him by starting the topic. She kept looking at him. She had never seen him so uncomfortable and nervous. For the first time in her life, she felt like she was in charge of a situation in their relationship. If it had not been so tragic, it would have been hilarious!

"Well, Sheetal I want a divorce," he said in one go as if something was weighing on his mind which he wanted to get off.

Sheetal did not react. Though she should have acted shocked and made a scene, she behaved very normally. This was perhaps because she was already expecting it and trying to control herself.

With an agonized heart and calm face, she asked, "Why?"

Sanjay was taken aback. He was not expecting such a composed reaction and certainly not a straight forward question. He was prepared for tears, reproach and blame, even for outright refusal to discuss the matter but certainly not this composed reaction with a one-word question.

He did not know what to say. She kept looking at him straight into his eyes. There were no tears and no reproach, just an intense look as if by staring into his eyes she could perhaps get all the answers that she wanted.

"Err, I guess I don't love you anymore," he said, avoiding her eyes.

"It's okay. I am not asking for your love." She continued to look at him with the same penetrating eyes.

"I am in love with someone else." This time he looked more confident and defiant.

"I know its Riya. So?" She asked.

"You can continue to love her, and we can remain married. I have known about your affair for some time now. As a mother, my concern is not for me but for my children. I cannot allow my children to go through the trauma of a broken marriage," she said. Thankfully, she did not sound as if she was pleading at all. Her voice was firm, and she sounded confident thought only she knew what she was going through. Her heart felt as if it was being bulldozed, and she could barely contain herself from screaming.

"I have to marry her, and so I cannot remain married to you," Sanjay said. This time he did not sound as confident as before.

"Why do you have to marry her? This arrangement can continue till our children are in college." She persisted. She immediately regretted asking him that question because she knew the answer in a split.

"Riya is pregnant with my child." The words were barely audible.

Her anger, agony, pain and humiliation got the better of her as she pulled up her hand, and with all the force that she could muster she slapped him on his right cheek.

She winced as her palm stung with the impact. She herself was shocked at her own reaction but more than that she was shocked with Sanjay's reply.

"How could you do that to me, to us? Do you have no shame?" Her control snapped as she broke down crying.

Sanjay too looked shocked, and he was about to retort in anger when looking at her face, he decided to keep quiet.

'It is too late to get it aborted, and I cannot run away from my responsibility, Sheetal. I have no choice." Sanjay's words sounded meaningless. Sheetal was going through her own hell to notice that Sanjay sounded more apologetic and guilty rather than a happy would-be father.

"What about your responsibility towards us?" Sheetal asked between sobs.

"You will still continue to be my responsibility. We can settle these things. The boys can remain with you, and I will provide for them." He was happy that she was in a 'discussion' mode so soon.

"What? How can you continue to look after their well-being if they stay with me? You will very conveniently forget about them because I will be with them. The boys are growing up. They need a father more than a mother. No, if you want to marry her, I will have to move out, and you can continue to stay here with the boys." She said as she got up from the bed. She suddenly knew what she had to do.

She took out her red suitcase, the one they had bought for their Manali trip. She opened her cupboard and put some clothes into it.

"What are you doing? Where are you going?" He asked, panicking at the sudden change in her mood.

"I am leaving this house for you to marry your child's mother and bring her here. Just remember that even if she does not love my boys, she dare not ill-treat them. My leaving the house does not mean I am leaving their lives." She said in a threatening voice as she locked the suitcase.

She took her car keys and bag from the drawer and looked at her husband of many years. She felt good to see the dread on his face for a moment. Yes, he would never have expected her to do this.

"Sheetal, stop". Sanjay now acted as he tried to forcibly stop Sheetal from leaving the house.

"Sanjay, do you want me to scream and wake up the children? I am also educated enough to know all the laws that support women, so don't try to stop me with force or you will regret it." Her voice did not even sound like her own. She did not remember when she had spoken to anyone in such a menacing voice.

The shock on his face instead of making her feel better, made her feel guilty for a moment. She thought of the baby breathing in Riya's womb and that moment of weakness passed.

As she walked towards the main door, she paused in front of the boys room. She wanted to kiss them before leaving, but she was not sure if she would be able to leave them if she did that.

"Bye Bye, my babies. I am leaving you only for your own good. Forgive me," she whispered to herself as walked out of the house with her head held high.

It was one of those nights when the moon decided to stay behind the clouds and torment the earth below by filling it with darkness. The path in front was not visible, but they were walking, more out of hunch, keeping one foot after the other, tentatively and cautiously.

Sheetal was walking beside Rohit, and suddenly he heard a rustle of leaves and a scream that pierced the silence.

"Rohit help," shouted Sheetal. Rohit could barely see her as she fell into a hole which led to an abyss. The hole would not have been visible in the darkness, but it was ready to engulf Sheetal in the split of a second.

More out of reflex than certainty, Rohit reached for her hand and managed to grasp it. He was lucky to hold it before she fell into the nothingness below. His heart was in his mouth as he knew that now her life was literally in his hands. He needed to call to get help as he did not know how long he would be able to keep holding onto her hand. But he also did not know how to get hold of the phone.

Just then his phone rang, but he was not in the position to take the call as the phone was in his pocket, and he was barely able to move. He was in a fix.

"Rohit please help me. I don't want to die. Save me, Rohit, please!" Sheetal pleaded as the sound of the phone ringing became louder.

Rohit woke up with a start. It took more than a few seconds to realize that he had a bad dream.

But his phone was ringing, and as he looked at the caller's name, he got goosebumps! It was so uncanny. Sheetal was calling at 12.30 during night-time!

'She must be in trouble,' he thought and with a feeling of dread he received the call. He was right. She was crying.

"Sheetal, what happened? Where are you? Why are you crying?" Rohit was getting worried by the minute.

"Rohit, I have left home and don't know what to do or where to go. Can you please come?"

"Yes, of course. Give me your address," he said. He was fully awake and quickly got off the bed to go out in haste.

When he reached, she was sitting in her car in the driver's seat with her head resting on the steering wheel. He opened the door and sat down in the passenger's seat. Seeing him, Sheetal started to sob again. Rohit took her left hand and squeezed it reassuringly between his hands. Sometimes a touch and a gesture say a lot more than words can.

Sheetal then told him about the entire episode. Even in the semi-lit car, Rohit could see the pain and the agony writ large over her tear-filled face. She winced when she talked about Riya's baby. Rohit understood that for a wife to talk about another woman bearing her husband's child was tortuous.

"You did well. One cannot live in a relationship without mutual respect." Rohit said trying to instill some confidence in her.

It was amazing how a completely confident, smart and a career-oriented lady from the corporate world could behave like an under-confident teenager when betrayed in love. A woman can fight any battle valiantly if she has the support of her partner.

"What do I do now? Where will I go? What will happen to my boys?" She looked at Rohit with desperate pleading eyes as if he had all the answers.

"We will tackle all the issues one by one. You can come to my house, but that is not a permanent solution and it might not be the wisest thing to do. So, we will set you up tonight at a hotel nearby. You need to sleep. We will fight the demons one by one tomorrow." Rohit made an unsuccessful attempt to make her smile.

They went to a nearby boutique hotel and got her checked in. After the initial breakdown, Sheetal was in better control of her emotions.

"Do you know Rohit? I have hardly stayed the night without my boys. I avoided official travel unless necessary. I had taken a break from work when they were young. I sacrificed my career to be with them and look after them, and today I have left them to fend on their own." The mother in her was accusing her of forsaking her children, but the woman in her knew that she had done right by standing up for her self-respect.

"You have not forsaken them, Sheetal. They can meet you anytime, and they can be with you any time they want. If you had allowed Sanjay to walk out, he would have gone scot-free without any responsibilities, which would have suited him. Now, he would know what managing home and work together means. Now, he cannot run away from his duties. You did what was right. The boys at their age need him more than they need you.

Sheetal nodded in understanding. It was amazing how this man always understood her moves and her actions. Anyone else would have judged her and called her a bad mother but Rohit had understood perfectly why she had left the house instead of allowing Sanjay to walk out.

Sheetal was also surprised that she chose to call Rohit out of a few friends she could have called up. Technically Rohit was not even her friend but a client. Circumstances had brought them close, and now, yet again, they had been thrown together.

Sheetal did not remember when she had last felt as comfortable with someone as she was feeling with him at that moment. Perhaps the fact that he was the only person who knew what she was going through in her personal life had brought him closer to her.

On an impulse, Sheetal went and hugged Rohit lightly.

"Thank you for your support, Rohit," she said. It was more of a sisterly hug than anything else.

Rohit too acted on impulse and kissed her lightly on her forehead.

"I will always be there for you Sheetal," he said with such tenderness that his eyes became misty. This was when he knew without a doubt that he loved this lady. It was not mere attraction, and it was not infatuation; It was pure and simple love. He could do absolutely anything for her without expecting anything in return. What is love, if it is not giving unconditionally?

He was in love with a married woman who was not only much older to her but also a mother of two teenaged boys! Strange are the ways of love! It neither listens to logic nor reason. It strikes at the most unexpected places and during the most unexpected circumstances. He was sure that she did not feel the same as he felt. Was there any future for him with her? He did not know.

He knew just this one thing that he wanted her to smile again. He wanted her to be happy. He would do anything that would take to make her smile again.

With cloudy eyes, he turned back and left the room.

If someone was to ask her when exactly she knew that she had fallen in love with Rohit, Richa would not be able to answer.

There wasn't any particular moment that she had realized that she loved Rohit, but it was a feeling that had gradually grown. Her feelings had changed from attraction to friendship and then to love. She was head over heels in love with him.

These days there was a perpetual smile on her face. Her day would start with wishing him on the WhatsApp in the mornings. She would wait for his calls. After talking to him, she would smile from ear to ear. Someone mentioning his name would quicken her heartbeats. After saying goodnight on chat, she would re-read all their conversations.

She had seen enough Bollywood movies to know that she was in love. She had confided about her feelings to her best friend Sonali who lived in Kolkata who had advised her to profess her love to him.

"Look, gone are those days when girls were not supposed to propose to a man. Tell him that you love him. Sometimes men get swayed by this. In life, it is always better to be with a person who loves you than with a person whom you love," she had declared as if she was an experienced grey-haired elderly aunt.

"What if he starts avoiding me after that?" She spoke aloud her biggest fear.

"Well, in any case he cannot avoid you at work, and so you still will have to time to lure him with your charms. Girl, use some of those feminine charms and seduce him. God has given us enough power, and we can have any man that we want. Only we should know how to use our power." Sonali had said in all seriousness, and it had made Richa roll out in laughter.

"Sonali, you are too much! With you around, no task seems daunting or impossible. I love you." Richa blew a kiss on the phone.

"Well, didn't Meneka seduce the pious sage Vishwamitra?" Sonali asked.

"But I am no Meneka," Richa answered.

"And he is no saint, girl." Sonali quickly retorted and they both broke into a laugh.

After the talk with Sonali, Richa had felt pepped up and in high spirits.

She felt like talking to him, and on an impulse, she called him up even though it was in the middle of a working day, and they normally avoided calling up during working hours.

The bell kept ringing for some time. She was about to disconnect when Rohit answered.

"Hello," his voice sounded as if he had woken up from a deep slumber.

"Are you still sleeping? Are you fine? You are not sick *na?*" Richa was suddenly very concerned as it was very unlike Rohit to take leave just like that.

"I am fine. I could not sleep last night and had some work during the day so I thought I would skip office today," he sounded awake now.

"Oh, sorry I disturbed you, then. Why could you not sleep?" She asked.

"No, no, I had to get up anyway. My alarm will buzz any minute now." He pondered whether to tell Richa about what had happened the previous night. Sooner or later, she would come to know anyway, but he decided not to say anything. It was entirely Sheetal's s call if she wanted people to know or not.

"Oh, there was an emergency with a friend. Had to go there in the middle of the night, and came back very late," he replied

"Is your friend all right?" She asked.

"Oh yes, she is better," he replied.

Richa felt a sudden dip in her mood and a sudden heaviness in her heart the moment she heard "she". So, he had gone to help a female friend in the middle of the night. She could easily place this feeling as jealousy because there was no reason why she should suddenly feel low when just a few minutes back she was feeling so positive and happy.

What did she know about him? He had told her that he liked her but that was all. He had never proposed to her. She was not his girlfriend.

But she needed to know where she stood in his life. She would have to divert her mind if he was already committed in another relationship. But would he chat with her or go out with her if he was in a relationship? She was not sure.

She needed to get some clarity on this and decided to talk to him frankly whenever she got the opportunity.

'Why is love so complex? Why can't God make two people fall in love with each other so that there is no pain and heart break?'

If only life was that simple! Richa sat brooding at her desk, not paying any attention to the file on her PC where she was making a business plan for a project. Her plans would have to undergo many changes if Rohit had already been taken.

Sheetal decided to take leave from work as she was in no condition to attend to official duties. She knew that she would have to get up and face the world but that would have to wait. She would have to allow herself some time to get over the shock and get a hold over her life.

She had not replied to Sanjay's calls the previous night and had later switched off the phone after reaching the hotel

He had sent a message that he was worried about her. "Let him worry! He did not worry about the consequences when he was fucking that bitch!" She thought with a fury that even she did not know she was capable of feeling.

Having an affair was one thing, but having a baby when you are a father of two teenaged boys was unpardonable!

"He very conveniently wanted her to stay and explain everything to the boys. Let him do the dirty work!" Sheetal knew that she was trying to justify her action of leaving the boys behind. Her heart was breaking at the thought of what they would feel when everything would come out in open. There was no way it could be avoided with a baby on the way. They would have to be told that they would soon have a baby sister or brother.

There was a call from the reception to remind her of the buffet breakfast. She did not feel like eating anything. Then she remembered that she had to call her office and switched on her phone. Her boss, Mr. Subramaniam listened to her. He felt that since she was falling sick so often these days, she should get a thorough check up, hinting that she was taking too many leaves.

She decided to come clean. Very soon, everyone would come to know anyway.

"Sir, there is some family problem. I will explain to you when I meet you." She said and thankfully, Dracula did not peruse it any further.

Rohit's call came through to check if she was fine and if he needed to come over. Sheetal thanked him and said that she was better.

There was a beep in the background when she was talking to Rohit and she could see that it was Sanjay's call.

She decided to take his call. She was not only his wife but was also the mother of his children. They would have to talk, even after their divorce.

She was already thinking of a divorce! She felt a strange uneasy feeling pass over her when she thought of herself as a divorced woman. She had often wondered how a mere paper could annul an intimate and so close a relationship as marriage. Now she understood. The paper never annuls any relationship. It is the action that does. Whatever their differences might be, they would still have a bond if this had not happened. This act of Sanjay where he betrayed the trust and faith of his wife had destroyed whatever relationship they had. The divorce paper would just be a formality.

She picked up his call and Sanjay said, "Which mother can leave her sons and go alone at midnight? Have you no shame?"

"Have you lost it Sanjay? You are talking of shame? I did not leave them alone; they are with their father. Don't you dare point fingers at me. I did not go and have an affair with another man, nor am I going to give them a step-sibling." Sheetal screamed at him.

The reaction was as expected. He calmed down a little bit.

"But you can't leave home this way. I had to take leave today, but I can't do this every day. They are your sons too. You have to take care of them." He was still not very subdued, and it sounded more of a complaint than a request.

"Where are you?" He asked.

"None of your concern," she replied.

Sheetal was amazed at her own replies. Previously, to avoid fights, she would keep quiet and never answer him back. Now she had nothing to lose and nothing to protect. Her world had crashed, and she had all the right to cause as much damage as she could to the person who was responsible for the crashing of her world.

"I am not coming home Sanjay. I am very clear on this. You have to take care of our sons. You can always take help from your new wife. Regarding visitation rights, no one in this world can deny a mother the right to visit her own children. So, I will come and meet them whenever I feel like it." she knew Sanjay had never even dreamt of this outcome. He thought he would leave and perhaps move in with his girlfriend, free from any responsibilities.

Thankfully she did not break down while talking to him. If she had not been offensive, perhaps she would have. She wanted to ask him where she had gone wrong. Where had she failed in her duty as a wife or a mother? She knew he would have no answers, and if he would say anything, it would only lead to mudslinging. She did not want to walk that path.

He wanted to meet her, but she refused, saying she needed more time. The only thing she wanted from him was some time to cope with what life had thrown at her.

"Sanjay, yesterday I thought I will not survive the night. The pain was so intense. Not only did I survive, but I also discovered that I have much more strength and self-respect than I had ever thought." She spoke to him as a matter of fact.

Sanjay, who was expecting to have to deal with a crying, hysterical and pleading woman, did not know how to deal with the new facet of this woman who had been his wife for so many years.

Rohit had taken leave to catch up on his sleep but after trying unsuccessfully for many hours, he finally decided not even to attempt it any more.

He got off his bed and straightaway went for a shower. A cold shower was what he needed to clear his head. His thoughts were in a turmoil. Now he could not use Richa as a tool to keep away from Sheetal. It was not fair to that girl either! She had called up in the morning showing her concern. Not that he did not like Richa. He liked her very much and loved to spend time with her. She was his kind of a girl, intelligent, smart, caring and spunky. Why did he have to fall in love with Sheetal? She was in no way right for him. There was no way they could ever be together. But after the recent developments with her husband's betrayal, was it really impossible?

He should not think about such things when she was going through so much pain and trauma. Looking at his watch he decided to look her up at the hotel in the evening. It looked as if she was totally alone. It was funny how women lost touch with friends because they were too busy managing their careers, children and husbands to find themselves all alone in the world one fine day. Women should learn to be self-centric which unfortunately most are not!

He decided to go and meet Sheetal in the evening though she had said it was not required. The thought of meeting her lifted his spirits, and he suddenly found his heart beating fast!

"Gosh!" He thought. "I am not a teenager, and I certainly can't behave like this."

He opened his almirah and automatically chose a mauve shirt, the one that suited him best and in which he looked mature.

He could not forget Sheetal's innocent hug. It had been pure and innocent, more out of gratitude than anything else. But that hug had sent shivers throughout his body. He had wanted to catch hold of her and crush her in his arms. He had wanted to kiss her face, her neck and her soft lips, but he had managed to control his emotions and give her just a peck on her forehead.

Love was such a strange feeling. It could make you passionate at one moment and tender the next. It could make you want to spend a lifetime with the person and yet accept the fact that in probability, she might never be his. He understood for the first time in his life what people meant when they said that 'real love gives and not takes'. He wanted to make her smile; he wanted to make her laugh, and he wanted to make her happy.

The first step would be to stand by her when she was hurting and grappling with the darkness in her life.

He changed in a hurry, but before leaving, he did look at the mirror again. Yes, he was looking good, but would she even notice?

He sprayed his Hugo Boss on his wrists and went off to meet the girl he loved.

He was driving when he received Richa's call. He pressed the button to take the call on the speaker.

"Hi sleepyhead! If you are feeling rested, can we meet today evening? I have something important to tell you," she said in her chirpy voice.

Rohit felt like a heel. He should have called her back when he could not speak to her in the morning, but he had not!

"Oh, Richa, I am sorry, but I am going to meet the same friend. There is some emergency at her end, and she needs me." He had no option but to say this since he did not know how long he would be with Sheetal. If Sheetal would permit, he wanted to have dinner with her. He certainly did not want to hurry back.

"Is it important?" He asked as an afterthought.

"No, No, it isn't," she said, pretending to be casual about it, but Rohit could hear the disappointment in her voice.

"See you soon, buddy," he said and disconnected the call.

Why could he not fall in love with her? He sighed as he shook his head as if disapproving God's plans of match-making!

It did not take him much time to reach the hotel as the office rush had not yet started. He gave his car for valet parking and rushed inside the hotel. He had forgotten her room number and he called her up.

Her phone was switched off. He went to the reception and asked the receptionist to connect him to her on intercom.

"Hello," she said. Her voice seemed to be coming from far. It sounded lifeless to Rohit, but it was to be expected.

"Sheetal, I am at the reception," he said, neither suggesting that he should go up nor that she should come down.

"Oh, ok. Come up in five minutes," she said.

He waited for ten minutes and then went up the lift to her room. He had a sinking feeling in his heart when he saw her face. He should not have left her alone. Her eyes were swollen and there were dark circles under them. Her hair was a mess, and she was wearing the same dress which she had been wearing the day before. He had a feeling that she also had not eaten anything.

He tried to hide his shock and smiled brightly.

"Have you eaten anything the whole day?" He asked.

She avoided looking at him as she shook her head in denial.

"Do you want to go down to the restaurant to eat or shall we order in the room?" He did not give her the choice of not eating.

"Let's order something, something light and also a pot of tea, please." Sheetal chose the easy option of staying in the room.

Rohit ordered two plates of *idli*, one plate *dhokla* and a big bowl of pasta. He had no idea about her choice.

As they waited for the food to arrive, Sheetal told him that she had spoken to the children when they had returned from school. Sanjay had told them that she had to go out due to some work-related emergency call. They wanted to know when she would be back, but she had avoided the question.

"What should I do, Rohit? I suddenly realize that I don't have any close personal friends. We have family friends, but they are actually Sanjay's friend's family. I was so busy managing my life that I forgot to have a life of my own as an individual." Rohit could see the hopelessness written large on her face. He wanted to take her in his arms and tell her everything would be all right.

He curbed his urge and just gave her hand a reassuring squeeze. "Sheetal, everything will work out just fine."

"I don't feel like doing anything, talking to anyone or going to work. How will I cope?" She did not sound like a confident, almost 40 years old woman but like an unsure and under-confident teenager.

"It's not even 24 hours. Give yourself some time. The one who gives us the problems, also gives us the strength to cope with it." Rohit just repeated what his mother would often say to him.

"Yes, I know." She nodded her head.

"Why was that she looked so vulnerable to him, and he just wanted to protect her from all the hurt? A woman, senior to him by many years, appeared to be so fragile and susceptible that he wanted to be her knight-in-shining-armor! 'Love and its strange ways!' He sighed.

They sat on the sofa-chairs as they had their meal. It was good that he had ordered enough food since both of them were hungry and finished off every morsel.

Later, they sat together talking. Sheetal did most of the talking, reminiscing and recalling the blind faith and trust she always had on her husband. She spoke about the personal sacrifices that she had made for her husband and her family, only to be thrown out of his life like a fly from milk!

A physical injury heals with time. A broken bone also mends and is as good as new. But to regain a trust once broken, is very difficult.

Trust does not die alone. Along with it, dies the faith in humanity and the dreams for the future.

Sheetal opened her eyes to the bright sunlight coming through the open curtain. She looked at her watch and gasped. It was already 8 AM! By now the children would have left for school and Sanjay would be getting ready. '*I will have to take leave today also,*' she thought.

After talking to Rohit, the day before, she had felt better. Her mind had also accepted reality even though sometimes she felt that she was going through a nightmare.

She had a detailed discussion with Rohit, who suggested they should look for a house for her to move into. Richa had recently shifted to a two-bedroom flat and Rohit suggested that she move in with her for a few days until they found a place for her. This sounded like a good idea to her.

She would have to go to work the next day. Now that she would be divorced, her current job would be necessary. There would be no man who would be providing for her, not that Sanjay ever "provided" for her. It was her salary that was used for all household expenses. His salary was used for paying the EMIs of the housing loan and for investing in savings. The house was in his name, and so were all the savings. It had never occurred to her to have any savings in her name also.

'*Women are such fools,*' she thought wryly. Not only did they love whole-heartedly but they also trusted their husbands implicitly and blindly. They truly believe that the relationship is for '*Saat janam*' and that the *karwa chauth* fast they keep for their husbands will always keep the love alive!

She felt a wave of bitterness engulf her mind but then she tried to shrug it off. She was feeling better than the day before and believed that things would certainly get better with time. *Time, they say is the best healer, but time does not take away the pain; it only teaches you to live with the pain, embrace it and make it a part of your life.*

Instead of crying and moping about her loss, she decided to take stock of the situation. *'Today, she would also go and meet the children.'* She would have to do the explaining as Sanjay had very conveniently avoided that.

She called up her best friend, Milli who had been residing in California since last many years. Milli was her school as well as college friend but after marrying an NRI she had gone abroad. As expected, when Sheetal shared what had happened to her, Milli advised her to file for divorce with a big fat compensation. Conversation with Milli was mentally exhausting, but after talking to her and Rohit, she had felt as if a burden had been taken off her. The weight on her chest seemed to reduce a little.

She quickly finished her morning routine and went down for breakfast. She had thought of ordering room service but then she changed her mind. She had to face the world. She couldn't be a recluse.

She sat down at a corner table and ordered a dosa and coffee. The buffet spread was large, but this did not excite her. The small pleasures of life also get lost when there are bigger problems.

After having a quick breakfast, she went up to the room to get her car keys. She needed to make a few calls. She needed to talk to Richa about the staying arrangements which would be only for a few days until she found her own accommodation. She could not keep her phone switched off indefinitely. She needed to sort things out. She pondered for a while, then sat on the bed and switched on her phone.

She dialed Sanjay's number, and he picked up on the second ring itself.

"Where are you?" was the first thing he said, but this time his voice was mellow and not as authoritative as the last time.

"It is none of your concern, but we have to meet to discuss things. Come home before the kids return from school and we will talk." She sounded composed and confident whereas in reality she was in jitters. It took a lot of resolve to remain calm whereas all she wanted to do was scream at him to let go of that heaviness that engulfed her heart.

"I am at home. I was leaving for work but now I will wait for you," he said. He was at a loss as to how to deal with a different version of his wife, a version that he had never seen before.

In less than an hour, she was standing in front of her own house. She felt like a stranger and her heart beat fast. She hoped and prayed that she would remain calm. She did not want to break down and display her weakness. However, much she was hurting inside, she would never give him the pleasure of breaking her spirits. If she did not matter to him and her sacrifices did not mean anything, he should also know that he had ceased to exist for her. He was now her past, a past with which her present would have to remain connected because of the boys.

He opened the door immediately as if he was waiting for her. She was shocked to see his face. He looked as if he had aged in just a day. He had not shaved, looking pale, and dark circles were under his eyes. Whereas one part of her was concerned but another part rejoiced at the transformation.

She had no idea that she was looking as distraught as he was. She had not bothered to look at her face in the mirror before coming out and so did not know this.

She sat on the sofa as Sanjay sat in the opposite chair.

"What is this nonsense about leaving the children and house, Sheetal?"

"Why is it a nonsense? If you leaving the house is all right, then why is my leaving absurd?"

"You can't leave the children." He tried to make her feel guilty.

"I am not planning to leave them. I will just not stay with them," she replied.

"Look Sanjay, when you impregnated that woman, you knew you were bringing another life into this world. How can you shirk your responsibilities as a father to the two sons you already have? They are boys and are of age when they need their father. Also, don't for a moment think that I am abandoning them. I will be involved in their upbringing as much as you will be. The only difference will be that we will not be staying together." Sheetal had done a lot of thinking on the subject and was very clear in her mind that this was how it would be.

"This is not possible," he raised his voice.

"Don't you shout at me Sanjay." Sheetal did not raise her voice even a decibel, but her tone was caustic enough to shut him up.

"Look here, it is you who has cheated on me. It was you who wanted a divorce. So, you are in no position to dictate terms to me. If I want, I can refuse you a divorce and your child will be born illegitimate. So just remember that I set the rules, not you, " she told her shocked husband.

"I have sacrificed my youth, my friends, my likes, my hobbies and my whole identity to be a good wife, an ideal daughter-in-law and a good mother. But when the time has come when I can relax and live life a little, I find myself alone. However, much you dislike, you will have to take care of our children. And beware, if I ever find that your new wife is discriminating against my children, I will make sure that you will have to answer me." She could feel the anger rising, a wild fury starting to grow.

"The children need you." He was now pleading.

"They need both the parents, and they will have both of them. Only change will be that I will be staying apart. If you move out, they will be abandoned by their father, I know. You will always have excuses for not coming to see them, and gradually you will drift apart. This will never happen to me. I will never be distanced from my boys, however far we may be. So, you can tell your girlfriend that she bargained for one but is getting three; two boys free with the one man that she wants." Sheetal made a feeble attempt at sarcastic humor but her laughter was muffled and much against her wishes, she found herself breaking down.

Sanjay stood like a statue, unsure of what to do. Hesitatingly he tried to keep his hand on her arm, but Sheetal shrugged it off.

"Keep your sympathies. I don't need them. You can give some to your girlfriend, because she would need them very soon when her boyfriend turns into a husband, rather, a selfish and perfectionist husband like you." She was now slightly in better control. Anger is a best substitute to hurt.

Sanjay, who was always on the offensive, finding faults, complaining and dominating, was at a loss. He did not know how to handle Sheetal.

"Look, I am sorry." He began to say something when Sheetal glared at him and pointed a finger. "Don't you dare use the word "sorry". Sorry cannot make things right. Sorry cannot give back my dignity, and it can't bring back the years which I have wasted on you. I am never going to forgive you, but because you are the father of my children, I will only wish you well."

Sanjay had the decency to look ashamed. Sheetal wondered at how the tables had turned. She was always the one who was defensive and saying 'sorry' to Sanjay even when it was never her fault. She would keep quiet just so that the nagging would stop and peace prevailed at home. She realized now that her desire for a harmonious atmosphere at home which would always force her to compromise had been perceived as her weakness. Forget others, she herself had thought that she was weak but now she had found her strength back.

"I did not want to break the news like this. I had planned to tell you after the children's exams were over. This pregnancy was unplanned and changed a lot of things. She is far ahead in her pregnancy so it could not be terminated also," Sanjay said not meeting her eyes.

Sheetal almost laughed aloud. Sometimes the most intelligent men get trapped by the oldest trick in the book. How could a woman be ahead in her pregnancy and not know? This was a rare happening and such rare happenings often happened in cases where the man would not be keen on taking the next step, that of marriage.

Sheetal did not say anything. It did not matter now if he was tricked into marrying her or not. The fact was that he had been having an affair behind her back. He had always tried to make her feel guilty of not being a good spouse or a parent and all the while, he had been neither a good parent nor a good spouse.

The next two hours were spent in Sanjay trying to convince her to stay in the house and take care of the boys, but for once no amount of emotional blackmailing helped his case.

Sheetal stuck to her ground. and told him that she would contest the divorce otherwise. She also clarified to him that the boys would not be sent to any boarding school. Sanjay knew that he had no option but to agree. For a moment Sheetal felt a surge of emotion for him, a feeling of pity. He would never have thought that the tables would turn like this. Sheetal had taken a lot of responsibilities off his shoulders, but now he would have to shoulder the responsibility not only of his sons but also of a new wife and baby. Then Sheetal remembered her tyrannical husband and she tried to quash the feeling. Women are funny creatures, they forgive everyone in the world very fast, but they do not know how to forgive themselves for their smallest failures or shortcomings. Every woman carries an invisible bag on her shoulders, a bag full of guilt for not being a perfect daughter, sister, wife or mother.

It was time for the children to return home from school. They decided to break the news together though she had wanted him to do it alone. Shashank's reaction was much better than what she had expected. Perhaps being the elder one he was more observant and understood things better. From his reaction it seemed as if he was already aware of the affair. Saurabh took the news to heart, and he started shouting and crying. He clung to Sheetal and sobbed, saying that he would not let her go.

Sheetal felt a heart-wrenching pain. Though she did not want to, but she broke down in front of the children and started sobbing with them. No mother would ever want to part with her children but she knew that if she did not, the children would be bereft of a father. They would never be bereft of a mother ever, irrespective of whether they stayed under the same roof or not. It was a sacrifice she had to make, for their own good.

Shashank showed a maturity much beyond his age even though he was only sixteen! He took his younger brother to their room and came out after some time. During this time, both the parents sat as guilty convicts awaiting their sentence. Sheetal was crying but Sanjay did not have the courage to come and console her. If he had known how much havoc this relationship would cause in all their lives, perhaps he would not have started it. Alas, if only people pause for a moment and think about the repercussions of their actions, perhaps many wrong decisions could be avoided. But in the whirlwind of romance, that pause for a moment becomes a distant dream!

In about twenty minutes, minutes that felt like an hour, the brothers came out of the room. Saurabh was in control now and went straight to Sheetal and hugged her. "Mom, you will not leave us, *na?*" He asked, sounding like a two-year-old and not the 14-year-old that he was.

"Never," she said, hugging him tighter and pulling Shashank with her other hand. The three of them cried for the family that was being broken, for the things that would change and for the person that they had lost. That person, on the other hand, stood there, not knowing what to do. If only actions could be undone and words could be unsaid, he would have done it then and there. Only, it could not, and he had gone far ahead on a path from where there was no turning back now.

It was Shashank who acknowledged his father but that too only to accuse him.

"You could have waited until my boards were over," he said.

Sheetal came to Sanjay's defense almost as a reflex action.

"Sometime things are not in our control, Shashank, try to understand this, but we will see to it that you are least disturbed."

They sat there, discussing about how to manage the new scenario. There was still time for the delivery, and they decided to wait until the baby arrived for the new members to move into the house.

"Look here, I know love cannot grow instantly and also forgiving is not easy. But you will have to promise me this. The lady who will be your father's wife will technically also be your mother. I am not asking you to love her, but you have to give her the respect that is due to your father's wife. I will be more involved in your life, perhaps more than before, but she and the baby will be an integral part of your life, whether you like it or not. The sooner you accept this, the better it will be for all of us."

Sheetal did not know where the words came from. Perhaps being right and fair is ingrained in one's system, and irrespective of the situation, that shows up in a person's behavior.

Sanjay, though shocked by her advice to the boys, kept quiet and all four of them, who were a family unit till a few days back, were lost in their thoughts wondering how the changed equation would affect their lives.

Days passed with the speed of a supersonic jet and Sheetal was too busy to even think over how her life had changed. Life had taken a complete U-turn, and she felt she had returned to her hostel days. She was staying with Richa. Though it had started as a temporary measure it was now more than a month that she had been residing with her. She had of course insisted on sharing the rent. They had settled into a routine which suited them both. Richa was not used to cooking and she usually ordered food from outside, but with Sheetal staying with her, Sheetal started cooking for both.

Things back home felt strange. Even though Sanjay's girl friend had not shifted to their home, but Sheetal made it a point to reach home on time, before Sanjay returned from work. She would sit with the boys and talk to them. Though both of them were on self-study mode, but she would still make it a point to oversee their studies. She would also plan the next day's menu and inform the maid. Practically she was still running the house, albeit remotely.

In the initial days, there were many problems from Shashank. He would beg her not to leave her whenever she visited them. She would try to put him to sleep, but he would not sleep to ensure that she did not leave. One day she had no choice but to sleep in the boy's room, because it was too late to go back to her flat, and Shashank was still awake.

Gradually with continuous counselling, Saurabh also adjusted to the changed set up. Sheetal also went to their school and talked to the class teachers. It was amazing how women immediately empathized with the ordeals of one another. She could see the sympathy and understanding in their eyes when she spoke about her separation with her husband. They promised to be extra careful with the boys and be on the lookout if they saw any change major behavioral change.

The office was a different ball game altogether. When she explained to her boss that she had separated from her husband, he instantly went into a counselling mode.

Why does every senior person think that it is his birth right to counsel and advise his juniors? She was not a teenager; She was a woman nearing her fortieth birthday! She was mature enough to decide what was good for her and her children. But no, he continued to counsel her as if he was talking to a two-year-old who had nothing in her brains!

Sheetal felt a temper rise in her but she controlled herself. She did not want to annoy him, because now she needed this job more than ever! Until now she had left all the finances to Sanjay, and had never felt insecure, but after her separation, the financial insecurity had crept in.

"Men will be men," he said. "They are like wild horses. It's the duty of the wives to tame them."

Even during this grim and serious conversation, Sheetal could not help imagining Dracula as a horse with the reins in the hands of his wife who looked like a baby elephant. She suppressed a smile and rebuked herself for thinking of Mrs. Dracula as a baby elephant just because she happened to be very fat and short!

"I teach the boys not do indulge in body shaming, and here I am doing exactly that!"

Dracula then started talking about forgiving a few mistakes.

"Well, well, would he forgive his wife if she were to make such a 'mistake' ?" She thought.

He spoke about the boys who would need a father. That was exactly her point! To ensure this very thing, she had not allowed Sanjay to walk out on them, rather she had walked out.

He went on raving about how a woman was incomplete without her husband.

"Really? What about the men? Are they complete without their wives? Or do they have a right to change their minds as to who completes them?" Sheetal wanted to ask him but kept quiet.

Her silence made it clear to him that despite his lecture for nearly the last hour, she was sticking to her decision to separate from her husband. This infuriated him and he made a nasty comment.

"It is because of egoistic women like you that our society is seeing failed marriages and broken homes," he said in an accusing tone.

She was dumbstruck at this direct accusation. She had intentionally not told him that she had squashed her ego and agreed to stay with Sanjay, even after knowing he was having an affair. It was only after Sanjay had told her about the baby and requested for a divorce that she had agreed for separation. There was no way that she could insist on staying with him when he wanted out! She had that much self-respect still in her.

Her eyes filled with tears, but she bravely pushed them back and replied in an unwavering voice with her head held high, "Sir, I am a woman. A woman also feels the same emotions that a man does. She is also possessive and she also has some self-respect. How many times will she sacrifice for her family? And why only she?

"Why does the man not think, before they go 'wild'? Does he have no responsibility towards the family? Or does he have a license to infidelity?"

The tears that she had pushed back had expressed themselves as anger and her voice was raised.

"Sir, would you forgive your wife if she came and told you that she was having an affair?" She asked him directly, looking straight into his eyes.

His face went red in anger.

"Mrs. Chopra! You cannot talk about my wife like that!" He stared at her and if looks could kill, she would have been dead that very moment.

"Sir, the mere thought of your wife being unfaithful is so repulsive to you that you lost your cool, and here you are counselling me to stay with him day in and day out even after knowing that he is having an affair with another woman?" She asked.

All her patience was torn into shreds and in that moment, Dracula seemed the epitome of all the wrongs in society, and she vented out her frustrations on him.

"Sir, I am human with the same emotions as that of a man. I am not a robot. I feel pain, hurt and humiliation too. Tell me how I can make all this a part of my life and continue to live."

Dracula was looking uncomfortable now, and it was visible that he wanted her to leave.

Sheetal picked up the files from the table and turned to leave. "Thanks for your advice though. I know you meant well," she said as she closed the room quietly behind her as she left.

"I had gone to him for some understanding as I might need some support, but all he gave me was a lecture on why I was not a good wife and mother!" Sheetal felt a stab of pain again.

"Why is that it is the woman who is blamed every time things go wrong in a family? Why does she have to be always forgiving? Even in *kalyug* a woman has to give an *agni pariksha* every time! When will all this end?"

She had no answers!

Richa shut down her laptop and put it in the beautiful cover which she had picked up from the Apple store. She glanced at her watch and decided to call it a day. She had to buy some vegetables. With Sheetal staying with her, she was getting home-cooked meals, which felt good. More than that, she enjoyed her company. She was less of a senior and more of a friend now.

When Rohit had told her about Sheetal's marriage, a feeling of relief had swept over her; even though she had felt sorry for Sheetal, she was happy that Sheetal was the friend who had kept Rohit busy. She had imagined the worst!

Being the kind-hearted person that Rohit was, it was natural for him to help her. The poor woman needed some support as she had no close friends. When Rohit had suggested that she move in with her, Richa had readily agreed. Though it was meant to be a temporary arrangement, both women were comfortable with it, and so Sheetal was not looking for a separate flat seriously. Moreover, sharing the rent between the two of them suited both.

Rohit would often come to her flat to visit her and have dinner. Sheetal would join them sometimes, and at other times, she would have dinner with her children at her home. There was a special bond between the three of them. They were friends despite their age difference.

Rohit respected Sheetal a lot, and she felt good that her love was a kind-hearted person. Things were moving in the right direction except that it was not moving fast enough. She could see that Rohit found excuses to come to her house to meet her, but he still did not say anything. 'I will have to take things in my hands,' she thought.

An idea slowly formed in Richa's mind. Sheetal said she would be staying at her home with the children on Friday evening as her husband would be out of station. It started as a vague idea, but the more she pondered over it the more she knew that she would be acting upon it.

Richa invited Rohit for dinner on Friday, conveniently not mentioning that there would be only the two of them. Rohit had agreed. She was thrilled that she would be spending some time alone with him.

Friday, she woke up in high spirits. She was looking forward to the evening. She was planning to order mutton biryani and *mirchi ka salan* for dinner. Rohit loved the dishes. She had also picked up a bottle of premium Rose wine for the evening. She went out of the office during lunchtime to the nearest home-store and picked up a few candle-stands and perfumed candles! She planned to surprise him with a candlelight dinner with just the two of them sipping wine and looking into each other's eyes, soft jazz music playing in the background and moonlight streaming through the lacy white curtains. The glow of the candles would lighten up their faces, but the sparkle in their eyes would be brighter than the stars in the sky.

God! She was so excited! Her heart raced on like a marathoner as she imagined what would happen after they had finished dinner. They would have coffee sitting on the couple-*jhoola* that was on the balcony. This was one of her indulgences. The beautiful brass *jhoola* had just enough space for two people or rather a romantic couple. After coffee, she would slide close to him, put her arms around his waist and snuggle up against him.

She was sure he would also want the same, and he would pull her against him and hug her so tight that she would feel as if they were one. She would lift her chin, and his lips would seek hers out. The kiss about which she had been daydreaming for weeks would finally happen. Then she would tell him that she loved him, and he would tell her that he felt the same way too.

She was startled when the doorbell rang, and she came back to reality from her dreamland. She got ready quickly and went out to greet the new day, which was about to bring happiness in her life!

She spent the day in a dream world, barely able to concentrate on her work. Once, during a meeting, Sheetal asked her if something was wrong as she seemed to be somewhere else.

Richa did not know what to say, so in haste, she said that she was not feeling well.

"Oh, in that case, you should go home and rest. Do you want me to come to the flat today? I can cancel my program and make some other arrangements for the boys," she asked out of concern.

"Oh no," she panicked. "I am fine. I just need some rest. Please don't bother to change your plans."

"All right, but off you go home and take rest," Sheetal said.

'Sharing the flat with the boss has its own advantages.' She smiled to herself as she packed her bag to leave the office.

Since she reached home early, she had all the time in the world to dress up for the evening. She wanted to look her best. She soaked for an hour in the bathtub in which she had put perfumed bath salts liberally. Then she went out to the nearby salon to get her hair set. The stylist curled her hair in soft waves and left the curls falling on her cheeks and shoulders.

After trying out many outfits, she finally settled for the turquoise blue suit that she had bought from Meena bazaar. The kurta was simple with a snug fit, but the dupatta was heavenly. It was the color of the night-sky with silver '*mukasih*' work. As she draped the dupatta around her, she felt as if the star-studded sky had landed in her arms.

She accessorized her outfit with a pair of Swarovski studs and a beautiful Swarovski pendant that rested perfectly on her cleavage, bringing attention directly to her perky young breasts.

She applied very light makeup - just a sheer foundation with a hint of color on her cheeks.

She applied bright pink lipstick on her full lips, accentuating the pout. Eyeliner and kajal enhanced her already beautiful eyes. She sprayed 'Eternity' on her wrists, cleavage and behind her ears, and finally she was ready to seduce the love of her life.

It is not the makeup that makes a woman look beautiful. It's the emotions that she keeps in her heart that bring about radiance in her personality. No superficial beauty products can ever compete with the beautiful glow that the thoughts of love, care and compassion bring on her face.

Richa was in love and her face radiated the sheer beauty of the emotion!

She looked at the watch. It was only 6 pm. She set the table for two and decorated it with two perfumed candles. The freshly cut flowers that she had bought found their way into the crystal vase that adorned the dining table as its centerpiece.

She decided to play some music. She knew that Rohit loved listening to Ghazals, and so she played Jagjit Singh. Who could be better than him in setting up a romantic mood?

She looked at the mirror again, assuring herself that she was looking her best. 'Why is it that the most confident of women become unsure of themselves when they are about to meet the person whom they love?' She thought. She would ponder on this some other time. Currently, she was waiting for the doorbell to ring.

'He should be here any moment,' she thought. He was a sucker for punctuality, and he was always on time.

Just then, the doorbell rang, and she rushed to open the door. She paused for a moment before the door and took a deep breath. She tried to calm her racing heart, and then with a composed face threw open the door.

Her heart had barely calmed when one look at him, and it started doing somersaults again.

"Hi! come in," she said.

He had a bottle of vodka with him, which he handed to her.

"For the beautiful ladies," he said, giving her an intensive look.

"Wow! Someone is looking gorgeous today. You should have told me that you both had planned to dress up. I would also have worn my party clothes." He laughed as he entered inside.

Her face felt hot under his gaze. 'Gosh! Was she blushing like a teenager?'

He sat down on the sofa as she poured him a glass of water. He looked at the room and the table laid for dinner. "Is there something special today?" He asked. "Is it your or Sheetal's birthday? Oh, by the way, has she not returned from office yet?" He was full of questions.

"Relax! It is just a normal Friday evening. I felt like dressing up and having a gourmet dinner and delectable drinks in style with a handsome hunk," she said as she sat down on the sofa next to him.

"Unfortunately, Sheetal had to stay back at her home as her husband is travelling. You will have to make do with only my company tonight." She raised both her hands as a sign of helplessness.

Rohit looked crestfallen, but it was only for a fraction of a second. He was quick to recover, and he hid his disappointment quite well.

"I am in good company." He smiled and relaxed on the sofa, sliding back on the cushions and propping his feet up on the side table.

"I will get the drinks. Let's keep the vodka for some other time. We will have rose wine today," Richa said as she got up to get the wine bottle and the wine glasses.

Rohit loosened his tie, opened his collar and closed his eyes, resting his head on the back of the sofa.

Richa's happiness knew no bounds. She switched on the music system and then got the bottle from the fridge and the glasses from the cabinet. The snacks were already laid out on the snacks tray.

She looked at Rohit, and he opened his eyes as if aware of her stare. A genuine smile of contentment broke out on his face. Richa looked away quickly, afraid that her eyes would give away the secret which her heart held.

The next few hours were bliss. They both chatted effortlessly. There was not a single moment of awkward silence. They spoke of their families, childhood, heartbreaks, dreams, and many other common interests.

They finished the bottle of wine and then remembered that they had not eaten.

Instead of sitting on the dining table, Rohit sat on the carpet and pulled Richa down on the floor.

"Let's eat here," he said and opened the pot of biryani and dug into it using the spoon. He gave the other spoon to her.

They finished the biryani and also the *'firni'* that had come with it. By now, Richa was tipsy, and she badly wanted to hold Rohit tight and kiss him. It took her a lot of resolve to hold herself back.

"Let's sit on the *jhoola*," she said as she pulled him out to the balcony.

"Look at the moon," she told him as she made him sit beside her.

"Which one?" He asked, looking straight into her eyes.

"The one beside you," she replied, pulled his head towards her, and kissed him full on his lips.

There was no holding back then. They kissed under the moon, forgetting all about the moonlit night outside.

It was a very long kiss. They both were breathless. Richa had never been kissed in such a way before.

It was Rohit who suggested that he should leave because it was past midnight.

"Stay the night," Richa said, desire clearly visible in her watery eyes.

"No, my mind is totally confused. It will be wrong on my part if I lead you on."

"I love you, Rohit." Richa felt like a burden was taken off her shoulders when she professed her love to him. She would not have to hide her feelings anymore.

"Don't you like me, Rohit?" She asked. "Am I not good enough for you? Am I not desirable?" She slurred, pressing her young curvaceous body against him.

"Oh, God! You are very desirable, Richa, but unfortunately, my mind is in turmoil. I feel very attracted and drawn towards Sheetal. I don't know what it is. Is it love or mere attraction?" Rohit said, feeling slightly better that he could share with someone how he felt about Sheetal

Looking at her crestfallen face, he immediately added, "I also like to spend time with you. Why do I feel totally relaxed and calm when I spend time with you?" He asked in partial honesty.

He knew he was in love with Sheetal, but for some reason, he could not admit this to Richa.

He could not tell her that he felt high with Sheetal even without drinking a drop of alcohol and that with her, he was always excited and never relaxed. With Sheetal, every moment spent felt like a gift and every day an adventure.

What he felt when he was with Sheetal, was that love? Or the companionship that he felt with Richa, the feeling of being on the same wavelength, the feeling of being understood and the feeling of contentment he felt with her was love?

He did not know, and he did not know whom to ask. Time perhaps would have an answer tohis question.

Rohit stood up, took his car keys, kissed Richa on her forehead and went out of the door, waving to her as he went.

"Goodnight, my moon, sleep well," he said as he went out of sight.

As she maneuvered her car into the parking space, Sheetal saw the other car pulling up next to hers. She looked at the driver; it was Richa. They were both late to office. Sheetal had slept with the kids at home the previous night, and Richa had left early because she was not well. Sheetal waved at Richa as she came out of the car and asked, "How are you feeling today?"

"I am fine," Richa replied without a smile, and by the look of it, it was clear that something was amiss.

'Perhaps she is in a bad mood because of her bad health,' Sheetal thought.

The day was terrible! An order from a client that she had been following up since the previous month had gone to a competitor. Then Dracula commented, "It was because of your fight with your husband that you lost your focus, and in the process, lost the order also."

Sheetal felt rage rise inside her, but she curbed it. She needed this job, and she could not afford to be bold and speak her mind.

She was fighting with her husband? Was he an innocent babe, a victim and she the aggressor?

She was shocked at his thoughts. Her separation from her husband had taught her many things. It did not matter even if women conquered the Mount Everest; they still would be second-class citizens. She was supposed to toe the line that her lord and master decided for her! Her lord and master could be her father, her brother or her husband.

Sheetal reached out for the jug and poured herself a glass of water. Sitting on her chair she sipped the water slowly as if with every sip, a part of her anger was doused. She looked at the unanswered emails on her system and also the pile of papers on the in-tray. With a sigh, she took the first file and started working.

She did not even realize that it was lunchtime until she felt the pangs of hunger. She called up Richa on her intercom, but there was no reply. She then called her on her mobile, which again went unanswered. Finally, she took out her lunch from her bag and ate alone. It was funny that Richa had not come to her office even once, she thought. Even though the previous week her reporting was changed to Mr. Raizada of the strategy department, she usually would have a couple of queries or visit Sheetal to keep her apprised of the development in her work.

She finished her lunch quickly and got back to work. It was at around 3 pm in the afternoon that Dracula called her to his room. Bracing herself in order to bear his snide remarks, she went to his room. She was surprised to see Richa sitting in his room. Her eyes were red, and it was apparent that she had been crying.

"What happened, Richa?" She was genuinely concerned. Was Dracula giving her a hard time too? She decided that she would have to risk losing her job and give him a piece of her mind.

"Sit down, Sheetal. Apparently, Mr.Raizada has harassed Richa, and she has come with a complaint of, umm, sexual harassment."

She noticed that Dracula was uncomfortable using the words 'sexual harassment'. Of course, it had never happened in her office earlier, the complaint, not the harassment. She remembered all the challenges that she had faced as a working woman, dealing with her colleagues and clients. During her time, there was no redressal, so there were hardly any complaints. 'Times are changing,' she thought. She sat down and looked at Richa while taking the complaint letter which was handed to her.

She read the letter with a grim face. Raizada had crossed all limits. He had a reputation for acting like he was God's gift to women, so the women avoided him. He must have thought that since Richa was an intern, he would get away with harassing her.

Both had gone to visit a customer, and on the way back, they had stopped for lunch. At the restaurant, he had ordered a drink and insisted that Richa also have one. Unwillingly, she too had ordered a beer. He was flirtatious during lunch, but Richa ignored him as she did not want to offend her boss and did not take the flirting seriously. She had thought that she would be able to handle it. On the way back, he tried to kiss her in the lift, and when she resisted, he threatened her by saying he would get her fired. He had no idea that Richa had come through recommendation from the top boss.

She read the letter and looked at Richa who avoided her eyes.

"That bastard!" Sheetal muttered under her breath. Dracula asked Richa to go to her room and promised her that the matter would be investigated. He waited for her to leave the room.

"Sheetal, I have called you to counsel Richa. I will talk to Raizada separately. If she puts in a written complaint, we will need to form a proper committee and follow the laid down procedures for dealing with matters of sexual harassment at workplace. We can not afford to lose Mr.Raizada. Competitors are already trying their best to poach him; such incidents will only mean that he would leave the company, which we don't want. Just because she is the daughter of a friend of Mr. Chakravarty doesn't mean we need to take action if she gives a written complaint. Your job is to counsel her and get her to change her mind about her complaint."

Sheetal could not believe her ears.

"Sir, do you expect me to ask her to forget the whole thing?" She was aghast.

"Yes," he had the galls to look at her and reply.

"What she is doing is right. I am sorry I can't tell her to do something which I feel is wrong." Sheetal told him firmly.

"Sheetal, please!" He looked uncomfortable, but he unquestionably was pleading with her!

"If you do this, I promise this promotion will go to you and not Rohan." Her blood boiled when she heard this, but she ignored it and kept her cool.

"This is wrong, Sir," she persisted with her argument.

"I know, but we must think of the company's future and, at the same time, take care not to annoy a General Manager. It is a very tricky situation, and that's why I have called you. I know you can handle it well."

He was now trying to oil her! Sheetal felt like laughing even though the situation was grim.

She gave him a reassuring smile. "If this is so important to you, then I will try my best." She said as she left the room

Upon reaching her room, she called Richa who was more composed by that time.

"He is only a few years younger than my dad," she said, "I never took him seriously. Perhaps, unknowingly I led him on."

"No! Don't do that! Don't go into the zone of self-blame. This is the mistake all of us make. We start questioning ourselves. Did I do something wrong? Did I lead him on? Was it a mistake? Was my dress inviting?

"If you blame yourself, the world will be justified in blaming you. They are going to do that anyway. People will judge you.

They will say all those things that you are now just thinking aloud. But you know that they are not right. You know that you are not to be blamed for what happened. That man is a lecher and deserves to be punished for misbehaving with a girl!

"Richa, I know what you are going through right now. I have gone through it myself. Unfortunately, I could not do anything except complain verbally. I am still ashamed of the fact that I failed the 'woman' in me. It's not a good feeling.

"I have been told to counsel you to withdraw the written complaint, but I will advise you otherwise. It's going to be a difficult fight, but you owe that to yourself and to all the other girls who want to take action but cannot because of the fear of losing their jobs. You are in a better position here. You are an intern, and your father is the friend of our General Manager. You must not withdraw the complaint whatever pressure tactics they might use."

Richa looked at her and nodded. "So, I am right in wanting him to be punished? Will it destroy his career?" She asked.

Sheetal put her hand on her shoulder and gave it a gentle squeeze.

"We women think of everyone else but our own selves." She gave a sad smile. "We have to change else our situation will never improve. Did he not outrage your modesty? Did he not violate your personal space? Did he not grope you with his lusty paws? Did he care about how you would feel? Did he care that this incident would leave a scar on you for life? Did he care that his actions would give you sleepless nights and that you would start questioning and doubting yourself? He did not!

"If he did not think before doing something wrong, why should you think so much before doing what is right?"

Richa did not try to hide her tears anymore. She let them flow unashamedly.

"Look up the 'Handbook of Sexual Harassment of Women at Workplace' on the internet today evening and go through it. You will learn what the expected behavior of men in any workplace is. It will answer many of your questions. Women had to struggle and fight a long battle to get to where they are now. The least we can do is to raise our voice." Sheetal was not a boss now nor was she an employee of the company. She was a woman who knew how painful it was for any woman to go through such incidents.

That day the two women were united in their common cause – convey to the world that they would tolerate no more injustice. Enough was enough! Today's woman was bold enough to fight her battles, and no man should be able to infringe upon her right to dignity and equality and get away with it.

'It's all in the mind. How you feel about life is the exact way life treats you, Richa thought. Life had been so beautiful till just a few days back. She had been in love with the feeling of being in love, and everything around her was just perfect. She had dreams in her eyes and hope in her heart. And then came that night, which changed it all. She came to know that Rohit did not love her and that she had no future with him. She was heartbroken. The world had seemed dreary and bleak. That was when destiny had also turned its back on her. The wretched episode with Mr. Raizada had taken place, and that had been the final blow.

Though the episode had shaken her emotionally, she still had the courage to write a complaint. She did not discuss it with Sheetal before complaining since she thought that she would try to dissuade her from writing the complaint. After all, she would think of her company, not a temporary intern! She was touched when Sheetal did not try to convince her to change her mind. On the contrary, she was very emphatic that Richa should fight the case and teach the guilty a lesson for life.

Within a few months of her corporate life, she had to face this, and if she lost the fight, it would be detrimental to her self-esteem, and so she was determined to be brave and fight the case.

Rohit came to visit them when he learned about the incident. They had a long discussion and then dinner - just like old times; only this time, nothing was the same. Her heart felt heavy and she felt a void in her chest every time she looked at him. Why is it that when you realize that someone or something is inaccessible to you, the yearning for it becomes stronger? Her love for Rohit had become more of a pain, and with this unexpected incident, life suddenly seemed like a punishment.

She needed a break! After giving a lot of thought, she decided to go back home for some time. She would apply for leave. She was an intern and could have quit her job and gone, but she wanted to fight her case and show the predator that women were not objects and that he could not get away with what he had done.

Sheetal's reaction had again surprised her.

"It's a very good idea, Richa. Mail me an application for leave citing mental trauma as a reason for which you need a break. This will not only strengthen our case but also give us ample time to prepare for it. In any case, if there is preliminary questioning for which you are required, we can do it over video calls."

So, she packed her bags and booked a flight for the next day. Both Sheetal and Rohit went to drop her.

"Keep your spirits high, Richa," Rohit told her as he hugged her at the airport. "You are not alone in this. We are with you."

'If only he were with her!' Richa felt her eyes brimming with unshed tears. She remembered a line she had read once. 'The only love that lasts, is the unrequited love.' She now understood what it meant. She would never forget him all her life. Time might soothe away the pain, but the love would forever be alive in her heart.

"Sheetal, I did not expect this from you. After all the company has done for you, you chose to side with that intern who will leave us soon!" Dracula looked at her accusingly.

Sheetal could not believe her ears! What had the company done for her? She worked her ass off, and all that she would get in return were appreciation letters. The promotions always went to the male colleagues.

Like life elsewhere, corporate life also was never fair to women. Women employees were already under the scanner. Male colleagues who would go for frequent 'smoke breaks' during the day but stayed back after working hours were considered sincere and hard-working, whereas the women who slogged at their seats throughout the day and left on time would be given stares and branded as being casual and insincere.

Sheetal controlled her anger and tried to remain calm. 'I need this job.' She reminded herself.

"Sir, I had tried to dissuade her, but you know how the youngsters are these days. She did not listen to reason." Sheetal lied through her teeth.

By the look of it she could see that he did not believe her, but he did not pursue the matter further. Things were getting difficult for her in the office. There was no respite in her personal life too. Just the day before, she had received a call from her son's class teacher informing her that his grades were falling; she had reminded Sheetal that it was a crucial year for him and that she needed to ensure that he put in his best effort to score a good percentage in the Board examinations.

How could she ensure? Not only was she a working mother, but she was also separated from her children. She was meeting her sons only for some time in the evenings.

After Richa left for Kolkata, she missed her. The pin-drop silence of the flat haunted her. Back at home, she was used to the chaos of having three loud male voices in the house, and now she was left alone. Earlier, she would crave for some peace from them, and now she craved for their company.

Thankfully she was too busy to indulge in self-pity. She knew that the case would have to be prepared very carefully, or justice would not be done. Her being a lawyer helped as she was used to the legal maneuvers.

When she had left the house, she had taken only the bare essentials, and later, when she had brought her stuff to her new accommodation, she had not got her books. She returned to the house, and from the storeroom, she took out her law books and journals. Not that she would need it for Richa's case, but working on the case revived her love for her original passion. She loved to practice law, but after getting married, she had to quit, and later, she had joined the advertising firm because that was what Sanjay had wanted.

"One should never have a lawyer wife or a wife working in the police force." Sanjay would joke. "Both can put you behind bars."

It was ironic how she had moulded herself as per his choices, and yet had failed to hold him back. Despite everything, he had still found reasons to go to another woman! Even with time, this thought always succeeded in destroying her self-confidence momentarily. It was not only the loss of a spouse that rattled, it was also the dent that it had made in her dignity, confidence and self-worth. Only a person who had experienced it would understand.

They were making things difficult for her in the office. She was being labelled as a trouble-maker, because it was an open secret that she had not tried to dissuade Richa from filing the complaint but had instead encouraged her.

Sheetal was so engrossed in going through her law journals that she did not hear the doorbell ring. A moment later, when the doorbell rang incessantly, she went to the door. It was Rohit.

"I was getting worried. I called you on your phone, and there was no reply, so I came to check up on you. When you did not open the door, I panicked!" It was writ on his face.

Sheetal was moved. There was someone to whom her existence mattered!

"I am sorry. I had kept my phone on silent because I was reading, and I got so engrossed that I did not hear the bell." She apologized.

"What are you reading?"

"My old law books and notes," she replied, pointing out to the piles of books on the table.

"Coffee?" She asked.

"Actually, I am hungry. Can we grab dinner somewhere?" Rohit could hear the rumblings in his stomach.

"Honestly, I don't feel like going out. I was planning to have Maggi for dinner. Will that do? Or shall I make something else for you?"

"I love Maggi," he smiled. "It's been ages since I had Maggi. But please make it fast."

"Just two minutes." She smiled as she went into the kitchen.

Rohit kept looking at the receding figure. Her smile did something to his heart.

Gosh, she looked beautiful and innocent. No one could guess she was a mother of two grown-up boys! After getting to know her, he now knew that she not only had a beautiful face but she had an intelligent brain too. She was creative, wrote poetry, had an impeccable sense of humor, and to top it all, she also had a heart of gold! It broke his heart to see a person like her doubting herself.

Soon they finished eating the Maggi with coke. They then made some coffee and sat outside on the balcony, letting the peace of the night sink in as they sipped the coffee.

"Rohit, I was reflecting on my life. It never had a smooth flow. My road has been full of twists and turns, as if I am driving through a hill station. I am sitting on the edge. Any slip and I would fall in a deep abyss." She laughed at her simile.

"Hey, if you are driving in the hill station, then isn't the view out of the world?" Rohit asked.

"That's what I like about you, Rohit. Always positive." She smiled and touched his shoulder as a reflex. Rohit was quiet as he looked at her with intense eyes.

"I like a lot of things about you, Sheetal. To be honest, I like everything about you," Rohit said softly. With his eyes never letting go of hers, he gently put his left hand over her hand as his other hand reached out to caress her face. As if coming to his senses at the last moment, he instead tucked behind her ear the strand of hair falling on her face.

There was an awkward moment of silence. They both could feel the pull and wanted something they shouldn't.

It was Rohit who broke the silence.

"Sheetal, you write poems. Why don't you try writing a book? Writing is an excellent method for destressing," he suggested.

"Good idea. I can write my own life story. I will change the names, of course." She sounded excited.

"Do that. I have many friends in publishing houses; I will get the book published." Rohit seemed relieved to be out of that awkward moment. He loved her too much to risk losing her to a moment of weakness.

He rose to leave after finishing coffee. At the door, as he turned to bid her goodnight, Sheetal leaned forward slightly and kissed him very fleetingly on his cheek. As their eyes met, she said, "Thank you, Rohit, for being my friend. God knows I needed one!" She softly closed the door behind him.

After Sheetal was in bed, she received a message on her phone from Rohit.

"I will always be your friend, and you don't have to thank me for that. At the same time, I want you to know that I want to be more than your friend. Before you get me wrong, I am proposing marriage, not a relationship. I know it's too early for you to think about all this, but I want you to know what you mean to me. You are much more than a friend."

Sheetal sat up on her bed! Another twist in her tale! She felt a strange kind of feeling wash over her. It was not a bad feeling. She had forgotten what it felt like to be wanted by a man. She had forgotten what it felt to be wooed. She had forgotten how it felt to be desired and cherished. Rohit made her feel all of those things.

She got up to get a glass of water and gulped the entire contents in one go. She felt hot, flustered and nervous! Gosh, she was behaving like a teenager!

After quite some time and numerous rounds of typing and deleting, she finally replied.

"I need to thank you for I am genuinely grateful to have you in my life. When God throws you in troubled waters, he also sends someone to bring you to the shore. You are that 'someone' to me. You are much more than a friend to me too. You are the twig of hope that I am clinging to in times of despair.

"Yes, you rightly said that it's too early for me to think about anything more than how to survive. One day at a time is my motto. I don't think of the next day too since I don't know what surprises tomorrow might bring. But even if that was not the case, you are too young to think of marrying a middle-aged woman who is spoiled goods.

"I respect your feelings. The right thing would be to distance myself from you, because I have nothing to give to this relationship. But I am selfish because I need you. Friendship is the only thing that I can offer you today and perhaps always. I will not mind if you decide to move away from me. That is what you should do." Sheetal sent the message with apprehension. She did not want to lose him. He was keeping her sane!

"Sheetal, age is just a number. I have never felt this way about anyone before, and I am not going out of your life unless you specifically ask me to do so," he texted back.

From the darkness of their respective rooms, they kept messaging each other till the wee hours of the morning, drawing boundaries and then breaking them – talking about their past and the future that they might never have, expressing their fears and failures, their dreams and desires and their loneliness and longings.

When God had created the universe, he had just created Adam and Eve in it. He had not made any rules, regulations, boundaries and restrictions. It was Man who had made them, because he wanted to have a society with systems in place. These restrictions are superficial; they are extrinsic. The intrinsic nature of all human beings is to seek love and belongingness. The heart does not know the rights and wrongs as it was not made to understand these. The heart just knows when it feels 'right' when it beats for someone else; the age, gender, caste or creed, nothing matters to the heart. Those are problems left to the brain to deal with!

Luckily for her, there was no awkwardness in their relationship after the incident that had taken place at her home. It was more than a week, and they had met twice, once for coffee outside and once for dinner at her house. If anything, their bond had grown stronger after the cards were laid on the table.

They discussed their office politics, their personal lives, Richa's case and Sheetal's book.

It was a Saturday, and she worked on her book throughout the morning, writing chapter after chapter. Then she went home to meet the boys for whom she had planned to cook kofta curry as they had made her promise during the week. Her family loved her kofta curry.

She was surprised to see that Sanjay was at home. They had lunch together as a family. Though she did not want to eat with Sanjay, she did not create a scene for the sake of the boys. Both seemed happy to see them together. She had spoken to Saurabh about his studies, and he had assured her that he would not let the family troubles come in the way of his preparation for the exams.

"Mom, chill. You are not the only parents in my class who are separated. I have many friends whose parents are divorced or separated. It's no big deal today, so stop worrying unnecessarily about us," he had told her. Sheetal did not know whether to be happy or sad. Were things so bad in society that children were not even affected when their parents separated? Sadly, the family units were disintegrating, and it was the new 'normal'!

It was very late, around six in the evening that she returned home, and after taking rest for some time, she went to the kitchen to prepare biryani for dinner. She was expecting Rohit, and they had planned to open a bottle of wine. After finishing her work, she lay the table and took a quick shower.

She decided to dress up for dinner and wore a pink top and a flowing mauve skirt. The skirt and top were gifts from the boys on her previous birthday.

She blow-dried her hair and decided to leave it open. She applied a light foundation and was in the process of applying lipstick when her phone rang!

It was Riya! Her heart missed a beat. She hated herself for being so weak that the mere thought of talking to the other woman scared her.

Taking a deep breath, she took the call.

"Why are you doing this?" She yelled at her.

"Doing what?" Sheetal did not comprehend why Riya was shouting at her.

"You are using the boys to win him back, aren't you? First, very cleverly, you went out of the house instead of letting Sanjay come to me. Then naturally, Sanjay could not act as selfish as you did and leave the boys alone. Now you are again using your boys to keep him away from me." Riya must have been drinking a bit too much because she was slurring. "This is certainly not good for the baby," Sheetal thought. She made a mental note to talk to Sanjay about it. After all, he was the father of the unborn child.

"Look, Riya, I don't understand what you are talking about." Sheetal tried to interrupt.

"You very well know what I am talking about. You used the boys as an excuse to keep Sanjay at home today. He was supposed to come. We were supposed to go to the hospital. He did not come, because he said you insisted that he spent some time with the boys!" Riya was now literally shouting at the top of her voice.

"Why don't you give a divorce? Why are you making my life miserable? I am telling you; I will kill myself and leave a suicide note blaming you for my death. Do you want that?" Riya threatened.

"Riya, how can I give him a divorce when he has not asked for it. He has to file for one. But we will talk about it tomorrow when you are sober." Sheetal tried to make her see reason.

"Don't act innocent, you bitch! You are a liar! You are clinging on to a man who doesn't want you. Have some self-respect. Stop chasing him, you slut. I am warning you." Riya slammed down the phone.

Sheetal felt her feet give away, and she collapsed on the bed. She was shivering and in shock! Every time she thought she was getting a grip on her life, it threw another curve!

She was the victim whose husband had left her for another woman, but now she was being accused of trying to steal him from her! Was there no end to the indignities that she had to suffer? What had she done to be abused by Riya? She would not have gone if she had known Sanjay would be home.

Just then the doorbell rang. Like a zombie, she got up to open the door and returned to the place where she was sitting. She was too dazed to even reply when Rohit greeted her.

She was still shivering. She was shivering out of anger at the injustice of it all. She was being harassed at work because she had done the right thing by helping a girl raise her voice against a predator. After leaving her for another woman, her husband expected her to take care of both the boys alone while enjoying his life with his new partner. The woman who had snatched away her husband was now accusing her of trying to steal her own husband and calling her a slut and a bitch?

She heard Rohit calling her name. She was seething and unable to respond. Part of her mind knew that he was calling her name and that she ought to reply, but her body refused to listen to her mind.

Rohit got hold of her by her shoulders and shook her forcefully. In that instant, something snapped in her, and she slapped him hard across his cheeks. He was stunned, and she came back to her senses.

"Oh, I am sorry," she said as the dam burst. She wailed like a child as she broke down on his shoulders and her body shook from the sobs.

Rohit let her cry even though he worried about what had caused this reaction. He cooed like one did with a child and ran his fingers through her hair.

They remained thus for quite some time till the sobs became less vigorous.

Rohit got up and got some water for her. She then told him everything. After the day when she had left home, today was the day when her control had snapped. She kept apologizing profusely for hitting him.

It was late, and so Rohit suggested that they have dinner.

"I don't want to eat," Sheetal said.

"Then I too won't, but I am starving." Rohit unashamedly blackmailed her emotionally.

They ended up eating on the bed.

Sheetal was composed by the time they finished. After clearing the plates, she went into self-pity mode, and the tears started flowing again. This time the tears were silent and not heart-wrenching cries.

Rohit put his arms around her as she snuggled in his chest. Neither of the two realized at which moment it turned from a consoling hug to something more. Their breath got faster, and their faces flushed. She wasn't crying anymore. She was a woman in the arms of a man who loved her.

Rohit tried to move away, but she pulled him towards her.

"Stay," she said, snuggling closer to him. "Make love to me, please."

"But you might regret tomorrow." He was not sure. Part of him wanted to crush her in his arms and make wild and passionate love to her, but the other part did not want to take advantage of a lady when she was most vulnerable.

"Rohit, I know what I want. I am not asking you to marry me. I am asking you to make love to me. And no, it's not rebound sex. I have been feeling this tension for some days now. So, you are not doing anything dishonorable." Sheetal was composed and sure of herself.

Rohit took her face in his hands and kissed her beautiful eyes, one at a time. His lips marked their presence on her forehead and trailed down her nose to stop at her lips. He could see her lips quivering in anticipation of the kiss. He lightly brushed his lips against hers as she opened her mouth eagerly like a child waiting for her favorite sweet.

Rohit put his lips on hers, gently at first, and then his tongue explored her mouth as the kiss became more intense. They both devoured each other's mouths, exploring, teasing and tantalizing.

They explored each other with their eyes, hands and mouth. Their lovemaking had the heat of a volcano and the coolness of a refreshing breeze. It had a raging river's passion and a silent stream's gentleness. Their lovemaking did not even for a moment feel wrong or illicit.

It is not a piece of paper that makes such an intimate act right or wrong. It's the underlying feeling in it which defines the act. That night a man and a woman silenced all the voices in their heads and listened to their hearts as they spent the night loving each other with mind, soul and body.

Everything changed after that night. If Sheetal had to pinpoint the exact moment that her life changed, she would choose that moment when she decided to listen to her heart for the first time in her life.

In retrospect, she realized that she had listened to others throughout her life. She had chased someone else's dreams and followed someone else's dictum. He parents had wanted her to pursue law; she had. Though she was not ready for marriage, but since they had wanted her to marry, she had. Her husband had wanted her to stop practicing law and join an advertising firm, she had. Her father-in-law had wanted her to cook at home and not keep a maid for cooking, and she had done exactly that. Her choices had never been her own. Her decisions were always based on considerations that were always for others. Whether it was a career choice or choosing a movie to watch, the decision was never hers.

Even when she would take any decision, it would always be affected by what others would think, do or how they would judge her.

That night, she for the first time in her life, had decided to do what she wanted, without thinking about the rights or wrongs of it. That was a decision she had taken as a responsible adult, fully aware of the consequences, and she felt good!

The change in her was very obvious even to others. The day she had accepted herself with all her flaws, the world too accepted her on her terms. The world is a mirror, and it throws back at you what you give to it. Also, the way you look at yourself is the way the world looks at you.

Never before had Sheetal been loved the way Rohit had made love to her. Lately, for the last many years, she and Sanjay hardly made love. Even during the early days when they were newly married, Sanjay was selfish in his lovemaking the way he was selfish in everything else. He would be focused on his pleasure, whereas Rohit's sole focus was to make her moan with pleasure. What she had seen in the movies and read in books was becoming a reality.

A part of her knew the truth. She had got married to Sanjay and had grown to love him because it was expected of her. A woman has no choice but to love her husband; after all, her existence depends on him! On the contrary, she was under no obligation to love Rohit; it happened slowly and gradually before she realised it. It was love that made everything so beautiful for them. It was love that made them focus on each other's pleasure.

Yes, she was in love with Rohit. Perhaps she had been in love with him for a long time but had not admitted it to herself.

Sheetal made it clear to Rohit that there should not be any change in their friendship. Forget marriage; she was not sure of a relationship too. She had to take a grip on her life. She had let people walk over her all her life; now, she was the pilot of her ship.

"Sheetal, we will only go as per your wishes. You call the shots. I will just follow." He had assured her.

After giving some thought, she decided not to get into another relationship before she was out of the current one. She needed to cut the cord with her past before she entered into her future.

If Rohit was disappointed, he hid it well and again assured her that he would always be by her side as a friend.

Sheetal had once travelled in the bullet train while accompanying Sanjay on a business trip to China. She still remembered the feeling; she could hardly grasp a scenery before it changed to another. The train would pass so fast that everything would blur, and she could hardly remember what she saw out of the train window during her journey.

She was getting the same feeling these days. Richa's case had proved to be more difficult than she had imagined. None from the office wanted to testify against a senior officer for the sake of an intern! Even the ladies in the company pretended not to know anything about the lecherous nature of Mr. Raizada.

The previous week Sheetal had been sitting in her office preparing for the next presentation with one of her clients when her intercom had buzzed.

Mitali, the Assistant Manager from Mr. Raizada's department, was on the line.

"Ma'am, if you promise not to bring out my name, I want to tell you something," she had said softly.

Sheetal had had enough of this. "Mitali, what good will your information be for this case if I cannot use your name?" She said, albeit a little harsher than she had intended. Even though she understood the reluctance of the employees to speak against a senior person openly, but if none decided to speak up, the culprit would get away.

"Ma'am, I can't testify, but I can tell you about a girl who might. Sanya had worked in Sir's department but had left abruptly. She was a victim of his sexual overtures, and when she had resisted, he had started making her life in the office miserable so much so that she had to resign."

Sheetal was all ears as she took down the girl's phone number. She immediately called her up, and it did not take even the slightest convincing for Sanya to meet her at a café to share her story. They met the same evening, and she narrated a story that was the story of many working girls, especially in private sectors.

"Look, I don't judge girls who are using their femininity to get undue favours or promotions, but not all are like that. Men do not have the right to assume that just because a female is ambitious, she will be ready to sleep with the bosses." Even though Sanya had resigned, she still had not got over the trauma and agony of being harassed.

Sheetal patted her hand reassuringly. Sometimes a touch conveys more than words do. Sanya narrated how Mr. Raizada insisted on giving her lifts every day in his car, and he would touch her inappropriately during the drive. In the beginning, she had avoided it, but later, she had to clearly tell him that she was not interested in forming any relationship with him. All hell broke loose thereafter, and he began insulting her in public, finding faults in her work and shouting at her for no reason. She complained to a senior lady who advised her to look for another job secretly and then resign. "No one likes trouble makers," she had said. "If you complain, word will travel, and getting a good job will be difficult for you."

She took her advice and found another job. She was lucky to have found one; everyone isn't.

"Even today, I seethe when I think of the injustice of it all," Sanya was deeply scarred.

She, of course, was ready to testify against him.

Sheetal also approached his previous employers since grapevine had it that he had to resign from his previous office due to some similar scandal. Slowly but steadily, Sheetal had started building a solid case against Mr. Raizada. It was more than three months, and the Committee already had had three meetings. They had taken Richa's testimony over a video call, and the hearings were almost complete.

With family, work and Richa's case, Sheetal sometimes felt she was on a bullet train again, wheezing past life.

The case was almost wrapped up, and the decision was to be announced soon. Even though Sheetal was sure of victory, she had tears in her eyes when she saw the mail. Mr. Raizada had been demoted, and he was issued a warning letter. He was also asked to write an apology to Richa, a copy of which would go into his personal file. This meant he would not be able to wipe away this black mark on his reputation by resigning.

Her mobile rang. It was Richa on the line. She too was crying.

'Thank you, ma'am," she said.

"No, Richa, I should be thanking you for trusting me to fight your case. I have always felt guilty of failing as a woman when I had not raised my voice when I was harassed at work. Today after years, I think I can forgive myself." Sheetal felt vindicated because if she had failed to raise her voice against the injustice done to her, at least she had done it for Richa.

"Whenever I visit Delhi, I will meet you both. I miss you and Rohit." Richa felt her heart miss a beat as she mentioned his name.

"We miss you too." Sheetal replied with all honesty.

No sooner had she disconnected the call her phone rang again. This time it was Rohit. He started off with a couplet.

"Dena hai ek paigam, Ki dil to rakhiye tham

Kyunki aaj takraenge jam, aapke jeet ke naam."

Sheetal laughed and replied in the same tone, with another 'sher'.

"Dharkane beetab ho rahi, intezaar hai appka

Jaam to mere liye, bas deedar hai aapka."

"Waah, you always outsmart me; I have met my match." Rohit was laughing now.

"Be ready by 7. We are going out to celebrate your victory," he said, and before she could reply, he disconnected the phone.

Sheetal smiled as she got up to get ready. She was feeling jubilant that she had got justice for Richa. She opened her wardrobe and looked at the dresses lined up. The black halter neck dress in front of her was the one that Sanjay had got for her a few years back on her birthday. He had got it two days after her birthday since the boys had insisted that he should get her a gift. Now she felt strange thinking how not getting a gift from Sanjay used to cause her pain. Till a few months back, she used to be so much affected by his actions. The sleepless nights, the wet pillows, the self-pity and the sense of betrayal were all real, but things were changing fast.

Her 'one day at a time' motto had taught her to cope with her pain, and her everyday struggle to survive as a single working woman was so demanding that she hardly had any time to brood. The episode with Richa had brought out the lawyer in her again. Her life today was 'happening'. She was getting to meet the boys daily, and the time they spent together was something all three of them valued. There were no expectations from Sanjay, which brought so much peace in her life.

'True, expectation is the root cause of all problems,' she mused.

She decided to wear the black halter-neck dress. It had been tight for her for the last few years, but lately, she had lost weight, thanks to her irregular eating habits. She had also stopped the 'emotional eating' habit that she had been indulging in at home.

The dress fitted perfectly. In the figure-hugging black dress, she looked very slim and young. She had also got her hair trimmed in layers which suited her oval face and made her look years younger. In fact, the other day at lunch, Sanjay had taunted her that living without responsibilities suited her because she was looking at least ten years younger than her age. Had he mentioned this to his girlfriend too? Was this the reason that she was behaving hysterically?

These days the thought about the two of them together did not make her wince. It had stopped affecting her. She had started to believe that perhaps what had happened was for her own good. For the first time, she was living life as she wanted to and not how others wanted.

The dress fell just below her knees, and the black strappy stilettos complemented it perfectly. She applied a light make-up and the matching diamond earrings and bracelets were the only accessories that she wore.

Her weakness was her red lipstick. She applied it generously on her full lips. As her lipstick caressed her lips, she was reminded of Rohit's lips tracing the contours of her lips with his. Her breath quickened, and she felt her face flush. Their lovemaking was volcanic. Even though she would try to brush that memory to the back of her mind, it would always surface, making her go weak with desire.

With her heartbeats quickening at the thought, she looked forward to meeting him. It was strange how their age difference had stopped bothering her now. Perhaps when you are in love, you see only what you want to see, becoming oblivious to everything else.

She swirled in front of the mirror. Her weight loss had made her waist look slimmer and her breast fuller.

"I can give competition to any twenty-year-old sexy babe," she smiled as she put some shimmer on her bare shoulders and seductive cleavage. She was feeling a surge of love for Rohit.

There is no age for human emotions. Love at any age is as sweet, and heartbreak at any age can be as painful. As we age, we try to act wise by stifling our desires, but our soul is ageless.

When we fall in love, we let go off wisdom and are happy being foolish.

She was pleased, happy and content with her life. She saw a missed call on her phone which told her that Rohit was waiting for her in his car. She took one last look at herself in the mirror and almost skipped her way out of the flat.

That evening was memorable. It was the evening every girl deserves in her life at least once. He had taken her to the most romantic restaurant — a place with open-air seating from where you could see the Qutub Minar. The start-lit sky above and the dim lighting of the place gave an ethereal feeling. A light breeze brought a whiff of jasmine from the flowering creepers nearby. Instead of the usual loud music, a soft and soothing instrumental music played, which only added to the mesmerizing aura of the place.

They were seated on a beautiful corner table behind the reception area, hidden from view and so, they had absolute privacy.

The view from their table was breathtaking. The starlit sky was adorned with a glittering view of the Qutab Minar. A man-made marvel enhanced the beauty of a God-made wonder. It was an amalgamation of two beautiful creative worlds.

"Rohit, this is so beautiful." Sheetal gasped in awe and turned towards Rohit to share the delight. Her heart skipped a beat when she saw Rohit looking at her intensely.

There was love, desire, concern, care and a torrent of emotions in that one look.

'There is nothing more beautiful in the world to me at this moment than the girl I am looking at," he said as he kissed her palms that were on the table.

He moved his chair towards her side and came near her. With a slight tug, she melted in his arms. She could hear her heartbeat run a marathon, and she felt like she would explode. She reciprocated with all her passion as he lowered his head to kiss her. She forgot for a moment that she was in a public place and not a teenager but a woman of 40!

"God! How I want you now!" He said and as if trying to take control of his emotions, he sat down on his chair next to hers, still not letting go off her hands.

She had absolutely no idea of what they ordered and what they ate. The only memory of the night that she would always carry in her heart would be the emotion that she had seen in his gaze and how it had made her feel. She had felt as if she was in a trance and things were just happening to her.

That night they made love on the balcony, under the stars, and she understood for the first time in her life that sex was not overrated. With the right partner and with love in the heart, it perhaps is one of the most beautiful creations of God.

Sheetal was late for office the next day, which certainly did not go down well with Dracula. It seemed that it was only when she would be late to office that he would want her in his room for some work!

She hurried to his room, and sure enough, the frown on his face told her that it was going to be one of those days when everything that she did would only ruffle his feathers.

"Now there are no lunches to pack and still you are late to work. What are you busy with these days? Fighting a crusade for women?" He taunted her the moment he saw her.

'So, that is what is still bothering him.' The fact that Mr. Raizada would have to write an apology to the whiff of a girl, an intern at that, had not gone well with most men in the office. Whatever they might say outwardly, Sheetal knew that in their hearts, they felt that Raizada had not done anything wrong. It is but natural for a man to get attracted to a woman. If he makes an advance, then what's the big deal? She should refuse and forget about it. They conveniently forgot that the man uses not his charm to woo the girl but his authority and power to intimidate her, which is nothing but misuse of power and position.

Sheetal had known that she would have to take such barbs and face cold stares from her male colleagues, but the smiles on the faces of her female colleagues made her happy.

She called a meeting of the lady members of the staff in the ladies' room during lunchtime. She wanted to brief them and also advise them against discussing the case with their male colleagues.

As she entered the room, she was given a standing ovation. A lady had taken Richa on a video call, and she thanked Sheetal with tears in her eyes. Sheetal gave a short speech urging the women to be vigilant and bold.

"Madam, I have heard that you have a law degree," Maya, the typist in the sales department, said.

"Yes, but I never practiced law," she replied with a tinge of regret in her tone.

"Madam, my sister is separated and is fighting a case for custody of her children, but her lawyer is not good. Can you please, take up her case?"

"Oh, let me think about it," she replied, taken unawares with the request.

"Madam, please," Mary pleaded. My sister's lawyer is trying to fleece her as he knows there is no man in the family," Maya said imploringly. Maya was herself a widow.

Jaya, whom she vaguely knew from the Finance department, had joined recently, and as she approached her, Sheetal knew that she too would be requesting a favour from her.

"Madam, I separated from my husband a few months back. My salary here is insufficient to take care of the expenses of my two girls. Earlier, he supported me financially, but now he has married his girlfriend, and she does not allow him to give any money to me. I need to take legal recourse but don't have the courage."

Sheetal was shocked! This was perhaps just the tip of the iceberg. In just a few minutes, she already had cases of two independent women, educated yet victimized. She should not be pointing fingers, for she herself had remained a victim for many months. She would perhaps never have walked out if Sanjay had not spoken about moving out!

It takes more than just strength to come out and fight a battle for justice. The biggest battle to be fought is the one inside us. Years of conditioning make a woman question her own identity. It makes no difference if she is educated and independent or illiterate and dependent. Until she does not accept her own self, the world will never accept her individuality.

Seeing other women reach out to her made her feel empowered and humbled. Just a few months back, she was a woman who had accepted her husband's infidelity and lost her self-esteem, and today, she was brimming with self-confidence.

One never knows what turn life will take!

Things were settling down, and she started working on the two cases she had taken up. She had also applied for a chamber in the District Court.

Rohit had persuaded her to start writing the book that she had wanted to. The protagonist in her book was a woman. It was her own story that she wanted to share with the world to inspire other women who were unknowingly victims of domestic abuse. Abuse need not be only physical. Without ever raising a hand, a person can break another person's self-esteem and morale. She was very excited about the book and had already sent the synopsis and a few chapters to Rohit who would be sending it to a few literary agents. Rohit was hopeful that she would get a good contract from some reputed publishers.

There was so much happening in her life that she had no time to think about the direction in which it was going.

After returning from office, she would prepare for the hearings. She would order food mostly from outside, but sometimes she cooked too.

She liked to finish her writings when the world was asleep. She found the light of creativity inside her when there was darkness outside.

Rohit had practically moved in with her though he would go to his flat now and then.

Rohit had also met her sons. It was his idea, but she was very apprehensive. She dreaded the day when they would have to meet, but when the day arrived the evening went of very well.

"Mom, are you going to marry, or are you both just in a live-in relationship?" Saurav had asked, and she was tongue-tied at such a straightforward question.

Rohit again saved the situation. "I want to marry your mom, but she is not sure yet. She needs time to think and decide, and I am willing to wait for her decision," he replied calmly and with grace.

She had not met Sanjay, but she knew that the children would have mentioned meeting Rohit. Sanjay would certainly not have liked it. But why should she be even thinking of how he would feel when he had not bothered about hurting her feelings for a moment!

Things were calm. The calm before the storm

She was in her office when Sanjay called. It was around lunchtime, and she was just about to start eating when his call came. She panicked because he never called her. They had assumed a stoic silence between them and communicated only through the children.

Praying that it should not be any bad news about her boys, she took the call.

Sanjay's voice did nothing to assuage her fears. He was in panic mode.

"Sheetal, Riya has had a miscarriage, and her condition is critical. She has been admitted to a hospital. She has no family, and I did not know who to call." He said in hopelessness.

"Oh, I am sorry Sanjay. I will be there in a few minutes," she said as she noted down the address of the hospital. Here was a man who had left his wife for another woman, and now that woman's life was in danger! Despite every wrong this man had done, her heart went to him.

She left a message for Dracula as she headed out.

"Family emergency" was the only excuse she could think of.

When she reached the hospital, Riya was in the OT, and a highly disturbed Sanjay was pacing in the OT waiting lounge. He did not look like the Sanjay she knew. Here was a man who looked lost, scared and helpless.

His back was towards her, and as she kept her hands on his shoulder, he turned towards her. To her shock, he put his arms around her and started to sob.

Even when his father had died, he had not sobbed like this. He was a broken man — a man carrying a heavy baggage of guilt.

In between the sobs, she could hear his mutterings. "The baby is gone. They are trying to save Riya. This is God's way of punishing me for what I did to you and the kids."

"Shhh... it's all right. We are all mere puppets in His hands. Riya will be fine." She tried to console him.

But Sanjay was sobbing uncontrollably. Sheetal understood that more than out of concern for Riya, he was crying out of guilt. A man can do a hundred wrong deeds and keep denying it to the world, but the day his conscience affronts him, there is no escape.

Riya came out of surgery and was brought to the room. She was under the effect of anesthesia and was sleeping. Sanjay looked at his watch and said, "I have a crucial meeting with a client without meeting her eyes. I will have to leave. Sheetal, can you please stay with her till I come back? I will arrange a nurse for her tomorrow."

Sheetal was aghast! She opened her mouth to argue, but he was already on his way out. She sighed and sat down on the small chair beside the patient's bed.

It was after an hour or so that Riya awakened. She naturally asked for Sanjay, and when Sheetal told her that he would be there soon, she turned her face to the other side, and tears started to stream down her eyes.

She gestured Sheetal to come near, and as she brought her face next to her mouth, Riya said, "Have you come to gloat over your victory? I lost my baby, the baby which was the binding factor between Sanjay and me. Now the baby is gone, and you have come to reclaim your husband, isn't it?"

Sheetal felt a rage so fierce that she felt like slapping Riya. But the anger was momentary because she knew that here was a woman who had lost not only her baby that she had carried in her womb for almost nine months but was also scared of losing the man whom she loved.

"No, Riya. Sanjay is all yours. I have not come to stake a claim on him. I have come to help you tide over this crisis. Being a mother, I can understand the pain you must be going through," she said in a calm and reassuring voice.

Riya started sobbing as Sheetal held her hand and stroked her hair. Tears were streaming down her face too. Tears are therapeutic. They heal as they flow. They soothe as they stream. They strengthen the soul as they slide down the cheeks.

Whatever their relationship and differences, these two women were tied to each other by the bond of sorrow, a knot of pain and above all, the bond of womanhood.

A few months after Riya's miscarriage, things started to change. Sanjay began to spend more time at home with the boys. In fact, during the evenings when she visited the boys, he would be at home. She tried to avoid him, but she noticed that he would often try to use the boys to engage in conversations.

Just the previous evening, the boys had been chilling at home since their exams were over. She was about to order pizza for them when the doorbell had rung. It was Sanjay who had arrived much before his expected time. The boys told him that they were planning to order pizza and asked him if he wanted one.

"Why don't we all go to Pizza Hut and have it hot and fresh?" He asked the boys. "We can also watch a movie later."

Sheetal felt anger rise in her, and she looked at him with disapproval, but he avoided her eyes.

What was he trying to portray in front of the boys, that things were getting normal? Their relationship could never be normal again. There was no point in giving the boys false hope.

"Oh, that will be nice! Just like old times," Shashank exclaimed joyfully before Sheetal could say anything.

Inwardly Sheetal fumed, but she had no heart to disappoint the boys.

"How is Riya doing?" She asked Sanjay pointedly, reminding him of his responsibility that he conveniently forgot.

"She is fine and is meeting some friends today," Sanjay replied, avoiding her eyes. After being married to him for so long, she knew when he was lying! She made a mental note to speak to him about it.

They had gone for pizza and later watched a movie together. Sheetal felt guilty about it as if she was cheating on Rohit and doing wrong to Riya.

'Come on! There is no commitment between Rohit and me, and Riya certainly does not deserve a place in my thoughts. She never thought twice before getting into a relationship with my husband.' Sheetal chided herself.

Even then, it did not feel right. Her relationship with Sanjay was over, and no amount of compromise could ever salvage it.

More than a year had passed since she had moved out of the house. A lot of water had passed under the bridge. The person who had left her husband and family to ensure that her boys had a father in their lives had metamorphosed into a different person - a person with incredible self-confidence, a person with a purpose and a person who now had her own dreams!

Yes, she loved writing that book. As words poured out of her soul, she was transported to a different world altogether. Words healed her; they soothed her scarred soul. As she progressed with the story, she realized that perhaps getting out of a loveless marriage was the best thing that could have happened to her. There was more to life than just being a wife. Every person had immense potential, and pretending to be someone else, just to please someone or to please society, was totally not right. Apart from being a wife and a mother, she was also a woman. If the woman in her was not contended, she could never be a good wife or mother!

Rohit had sent a few sample chapters of her book to literary agents, and a couple of them had responded. Very soon, they would be meeting to take it further.

Meanwhile, Sheetal had also started working on the few court cases she had taken to help her colleagues. From their reference, she got other cases too. All her clients were women.

Law was her first love, and she started working on the cases. They were not just cases for her. They were real women whose lives had been destroyed by their family members! They were battered women, defeated women, abused women and traumatized women - women who needed sensitivity and healing more than justice.

There were so many things going on in her life that she barely had time to think. Of course, she knew that very soon she would have to decide about her job. Because of her husband, she had taken up the job outside her domain, but gradually, she had started enjoying it. More importantly, the cheque at the end of each month made it worthwhile. Quitting her job for a law practice, the success of which she was not sure of, was a significant risk. She needed the money; she did not have a husband to look after her. He was technically still her husband, but he had never offered financial support, nor had she asked for any.

She often wondered why he had still not asked her for a divorce. She put herself in Riya's shoes, which certainly was not a comfortable place to be. After losing her baby, was she also about to lose her lover? This thought made her fume! The injustice of it all left her aghast!

Sanjay had not only destroyed her marriage, but he had destroyed Riya's life too!

Surprisingly, she did not feel any bitterness towards Riya. On the contrary, she could empathize with her. The feeling of being used by a man leaves a bitter taste in the mouth. She knew it only too well. After all, didn't Sanjay use her too?

Richa took a deep breath, trying to calm down. Her heart was beating so fast that she felt she had run a marathon. However, she had just alighted from the plane and was on the bus to the arrival terminal of Indira Gandhi International Airport, Delhi.

She looked at Rohit's message on her phone for the hundredth time.

"Can't wait to see you. Come soon." The message read.

He would be there at the airport to pick her up and take her to her flat.

"Why does loving someone hurt so much?" She asked herself yet again. In the few months that she had been in Kolkata, she had somehow taken control of herself and tried not to think of Rohit. They did talk on the phone now and then. It mainly was Rohit who would call, and it was mostly about Sheetal that he would talk. He had opened up to her about Sheetal, and perhaps she was the only one to whom he had spoken about it. So, whenever he felt insecure or was in pain, he would call her up to talk to her.

Richa never gave him the slightest hint that she was still in love with him. It was ironical that she, who was pining for him, was the one who had to listen to him pining for someone else. Sometimes men could be so insensitive.

'Perhaps he does not even remember that I professed my love for him. Or, he thinks that I am over him now,' Richa thought ruefully!

If only love could be switched off with a button, life would be so much easier.

She dragged her bag as she alighted from the bus, and instead of walking towards the exit, she walked towards the restroom.

'He might not even notice, but I need to look my best,' she thought.

After powdering her nose and brightening her lipstick, she felt much better equipped to meet the man she loved but who did not love her.

When she saw Rohit, she extended her hand for a shake, but he grabbed her by her arm and hugged her tight. Perhaps all those calls, during which he had poured his heart out talking about his feelings for Sheetal, had brought them closer than they had ever been before.

"I missed you," he said.

It was a simple friendly admission, but it sent her heart aflutter.

"How is Sheetal?" She asked, perhaps as a reminder to herself about her presence in his life.

"She is fine. A little too busy these days. After the miscarriage of her husband's girlfriend, she has started spending more time at home," he replied casually. It was perhaps too casual because she could sense a hint of insecurity in his words.

Love does strange things to people. Sometimes it makes a timid and an introvert person very confident, and at other times, it makes the most confident person doubtful and insecure.

Some time ago, he had called up to tell her that Sheetal had gone out with her family for dinner and movie. He had not hidden his disappointment when he had told her about the dinner.

"It is her life. I know that, but I think it will be a mistake if she goes back to the man who had left her shattered and broken," he had told her.

"But Rohit, it was just one evening. Apart from being her husband, he is also the father of her boys, so for their sake, she might have to meet him and go with him as a family. If you let it affect you, then you are in for a difficult time," she had chided him.

"No. No. I am fine. It doesn't affect me. It is not that we are a couple with commitments. Sheetal is free to do what she feels is right," Rohit said. She could sense the dejection in his tone from across thousands of miles.

As the car entered the colony, Rohit turned towards her

"Richa, in the last few months, I have shared my thoughts and feelings with you. You know how deeply I love Sheetal. You know how emotional I am about her, but please don't tell Sheetal anything about this. I don't want to put any pressure on her." Rohit caught hold of her palms with his left hand since his right hand was on the steering wheel.

Richa felt a surge of emotion wash through her. She wanted to hug him there, take him in her arms and assure him that everything would be fine. Instead, she just squeezed his hand.

"Don't worry. Sheetal will not know," she said as she brushed away the single drop that trickled down the corner of her eyes.

She used to think that "real love" was found only in books and movies; now, she knew that loving someone meant putting that person's happiness and well-being before yours. This was what Rohit was doing, and this was what she was doing.

If she ever confessed that she was perhaps more in love with him than ever before, that she pined to be with him, that her heart broke every time he took Sheetal's name, he would stop speaking about Sheetal with her.

So, she did not tell him; he needed someone to vent his feelings. He needed a shoulder to lean on, and she would gladly give him that shoulder even though her heart would break every time she saw him pining for another woman.

"Dear God, next time you make love-matches sitting above, make sure not to make love triangles," she complained.

The musical ringtone of her mobile phone woke her up even before the morning alarm rang.

'Who could be calling at this hour?' Sheetal thought with trepidation. Today was Sunday, and even though she had a lot to do, she planned to catch up on her sleep.

Richa had arrived from Kolkata the previous day, and they had all gone for dinner. They had a lovely time after ages. However, Richa looked a little tense and was very quiet. Sheetal assumed that perhaps Richa was reminded of her unpleasant sexual harassment experience since her return to Delhi. Such incidents have far-reaching effects; she knew it only too well.

Sheetal pulled out the phone from under the pillow and looked at the caller's name with groggy eyes.

'Why was Sanjay calling this early? Were the boys alright?' Sheetal experienced a moment of pure panic as she answered the call.

"What happened? Are the boys fine?" She heard herself scream into the mouthpiece, but in reality, her voice had come out as a whisper.

"They are fine. Don't panic, Sheetal," Sanjay scolded in a tone she remembered only too well.

"Well, then why are you calling so early?" She replied, relieved and a little annoyed.

"Well, I could not sleep the whole night, Sheetal. I need to talk to you. Would you please come home today? Make your famous Biryani, and we will talk after lunch," he said.

"Sanjay, I am very busy today." Sheetal felt her temper rising. Despite all that had transpired, he expected her to be at his beck and call!

"What kind of mother are you if you don't have time for your children?" Sanjay demanded and immediately realized his mistake.

Before she could retort, he apologized, "Ok, ok, I am sorry. I know you are a good mother. It's me who has not been a good father and a good husband. Please, come today. I have to discuss something important about our children."

Sanjay was again up to his usual tactics. He could be very sweet, gentle and charming when he wanted to get his way, and currently, it was clear that he wanted her to be at home.

"I have already told the boys that you will be coming home for lunch today, and they are looking forward to it." Sanjay played his trump card.

Sheetal felt rage rising inside her, but she controlled it. She did not want to get into a verbal duel with Sanjay first thing in the morning. She made a mental note to talk to him about this blackmail technique that he often used. He was using her sons to make her do things that he wanted her to do.

When she reached her house, Shashank had gone for his day-long tuition, and Saurav was still sleeping. She could have kicked herself for believing Sanjay's lies. However, since she was there, she went to the kitchen and started preparing Biryani. It was after she had finished making Biryani and was cleaning the kitchen slab that Sanjay came and hugged her from behind.

His touch felt like an electric shock, and she pushed his hand away. "How dare you touch me?" She screamed.

"Ok. Ok. Calm down," Sanjay said as if speaking to a child throwing tantrums. "I am your husband, Sheetal. It is not that I am touching you for the first time." He mocked her.

Even though she was fuming inwardly, she managed to keep a calm exterior as she said, "You ceased being my husband the moment you entered into a relationship with someone else."

"Did you ask me to come here to remind me of your rights as a husband?" She glared at him.

"Have a seat," he said again, trying to pull her by her hands towards the living room.

"Do not touch me." She looked at him straight into his eyes and spoke very firmly.

Sanjay got the message this time as he took a chair and sat some distance away from Sheetal who sat on the sofa chair.

"Sheetal, I have called you here to apologize. I know I have wronged you and the boys, but now I am truly and genuinely sorry. I request you to please forgive me and come home," he said as if he was apologizing for some minor mistake and not for wrecking so many lives.

Sheetal wanted to retort back, but she kept quiet and let him finish what he had to say to her.

"I have realized my mistake, and I know that you and the boys need me, and I am not going to run away from my responsibilities," he said.

Sheetal felt like laughing. Even now, he felt that he was doing them a favour by apologizing and asking her to come back.

"What about Riya?" She asked quietly. She was just curious to see his reaction.

"Well, after the miscarriage, our relationship is almost over, and I promise you that I will severe my ties with her. I have already got her fired from my company." Sanjay said without even a tinge of remorse in his voice.

Sheetal felt a wave of pity for Riya! Poor girl! Not only had she lost a baby but she had also lost her job and her lover.

Sheetal looked at Sanjay and wondered how she had remained married to this self-centered bastard for so many years! He had no remorse for what he had done to either Sheetal or Riya. It now suited him to have her back so that he did not have to look after the household. He wanted his wife back so that she would take all the responsibilities off his shoulders. There was no longer a baby to bind him to Riya, and so conveniently, he had gotten rid of her!

"You got her fired? Wow, so very gallant of you! You did this to ensure that I feel secure, right?" She asked.

"Yes, of course. I will remain loyal and faithful to you. You need not worry about it. I will never leave you again." Sanjay tried to convince her.

"Sanjay, you are forgetting something. You did not leave me. You wanted to have a wife and a mistress both, but I left you so that you did not shirk from your responsibilities as a father."

"What difference does it make? Things are fine now. We can go back to where we were before all this unpleasantness happened." Sanjay sounded perplexed.

"Unpleasantness? This is all that it was to you? You have wrecked one life, and you call it unpleasantness?" Sheetal could not control her anger anymore.

"Sheetal, I am sorry. I will make your life beautiful again." Sanjay grabbed her hands lying in her lap and squeezed them.

'How can a person be so vain?' She wondered.

"Sanjay, I am not talking about myself. You have wrecked Riya's life. You used her and now you have discarded her. Not only this, you got her fired too!

"You did not wreck my life, though I thought you had for some time. Now I know better; rather, I am grateful to you. It is only because of you that I have realized that it is possible to live as a woman and a mother. Were it not for you, I would not have met this confident and complete woman that is me."

Sanjay looked more perplexed than ever. "I don't understand. Don't you want things to be normal again, Sheetal?"

"Things are normal for me, Sanjay. Initially, I thought I would not be able to take care of our boys if you disappeared from our lives. Now I know better. I am fully capable of taking care of myself as well as our children without your help. Of course, you are their father, and they are as much yours as mine, but I do not need to be married to you for you to take their responsibility.

"I was waiting for you to file for divorce, but since you won't, I will. I have someone in my life, and I want to be free from this relationship before thinking of the future."

Sanjay looked shell-shocked. Never in his wildest imagination had he thought that this could happen! She felt a twinge of pity for a moment, but then she remembered how he had used Riya, and all her sympathy vanished into thin air.

Sanjay was quiet for a long time as if fighting a battle within.

"I will forgive your infidelity and put it behind us. I am willing to give you another chance, for the sake of our children," he said as if she had committed murder and he, in his benevolence, was forgiving her!

'Some people will never change,' she thought.

"No, Sanjay, I will not come back. For our children's sake, I will not be in a relationship where there is no mutual love and respect," she said honestly.

He tried to convince her, cajole her and even threatened her, but she held her ground.

She did not feel victorious; instead, she felt free and unburdened as she left her home that evening. It was the closing of a chapter and the beginning of a new phase in her life. She was free from a relationship that had tied her down, chained her and had put a cloak over her own identity. For the first time in her life, she felt she had wings and that she could fly!

"What I thought was the end, my plight

Was the take-off point of my flight!"

Sheetal smiled as she drove on. Her journey was just starting.

Six months later:

Sheetal was sitting in her small office. She was lost in the case-file that she was reading. This case had come to her only the day before. Her client was a young 21-year-old girl who had broken off from an abusive relationship. But now, her boyfriend was stalking, blackmailing and threatening her. It had taken immense courage on her part to come out and file a case against her stalker and tormentor. Sheetal could not afford to make any mistake as a life was at stake.

Sheetal was now gathering popularity as a feminist lawyer after she had won a couple of tricky cases for her abused female clients. She had started an NGO called "She for Her". Initially, she had started it alone, but later, two like-minded lady-lawyers had joined her. They were taking up cases of oppressed and victimized women who could not afford expensive lawyers to fight their cases. They had also managed to get some donations for the cause. They were making slow but steady progress.

Even though she had resigned from her job, she was always short on time. There was so much to do.

There was a newfound purpose in her life, and she had never felt more alive!

Even her career in writing had taken off with a bang! A leading publisher had published her book, and they had given her a contract for two more books. She could never have imagined that the two things which she loved doing, fighting for justice and writing from her heart, would bring her name, fame and money! She had appeared for numerous magazines and newspapers interviews when her book became a national bestseller within a month of getting published.

Whenever she was asked if it was her own story that she had written about, she would always reply with the same answer.

"It is the story of the thousands of nameless and faceless women all around us who suffer physical and emotional abuse from their own families."

On her personal front too, things were looking bright. Rohit had proposed to her again, and she had asked for some more time from him. Sometime back when Richa had come to Delhi, she had told her of the extent of Rohit's love for her.

"Sheetal, you are fortunate to have found him. His love for you is the purest kind, the kind in which one only wants to give, in which one puts the other before self and the kind you read about in books. You will be a fool to let him go, and I know you are not one. Hold on to him. Marry him."

Not that she needed to be told about the extent of his love for her. She could see it in his eyes and his actions.

She knew that she loved him too. She knew her answer to his marriage proposal would be a 'yes'. But before committing to a relationship, she wanted to close the old chapter and spend some more time with her newly discovered friend, the woman in the mirror!

She had filed for divorce, and Sanjay had not contested. Both her sons had also accepted it very sportingly. They had never seen their mother this happy and contended. They also got along very well with Rohit, who despite his young age, surprisingly behaved in a fatherly way with them, fatherly as well as friendly, and it was a perfect combination. She would take custody of her boys with enough visitation rights for Sanjay. She wanted her boys to grow up with both parents, even if they did not live under the same roof as a family.

'Life could not have been better than this.' Sheetal gave a contented sigh as she closed the file she was reading. She looked at the wall clock. It was around three pm; she thought of going home early, relaxing with a cup of tea and her laptop, and working on her next story.

Just then, the doorbell rang. The peon had already left as he had some work, and the door was also open.

"Come in," she said, wondering who it could be. She had no appointments.

To her surprise, it was Riya.

She had not met her after that day in the hospital. Riya had changed drastically. She had dark hollows under her eyes and her face had lost colour. She looked visibly aged and defeated!

"How are you, Riya? You don't look good," she said gently, offering the chair opposite her.

"How do you expect me to be?" She sounded bitter as she sat down in the chair.

'Your choices can change the course of your life,' Sheetal thought, but she did not say anything.

As if reading her mind, Riya replied, "I should have known better when I entered into a relationship with a married man. I destroyed your family life, and now, my life is destroyed too," she said, filled with remorse.

"No, Riya, we are mere puppets in His hands." She tried to make her feel better.

"Sheetal, human beings are such manipulative beings; we blame our destiny when our choices shape our future.

"I made the wrong choice, and I am paying a heavy price for it. My heart is broken. I lost not only my baby but my health and livelihood. My faith is shattered, my reputation is in tatters, and my self-esteem is gone; I am just a wreck of the woman I used to be. This is my punishment for doing you wrong."

Sheetal tried to comfort her, but Riya silenced her.

"Let me finish what I have come to say, Sheetal. It took me a lot of courage to come here. Please just hear me out.

"I know I have erred, and I paid a huge price for it. What makes me furious is the injustice of it all. Sanjay used me and now has discarded me like an old pair of jeans! He got me fired. Why? Because it did not suit him to see my face daily. He could have quit the job; he could have easily found another. But with the stigma attached to my name, I am not getting any respectable job.

"So, after a lot of thinking, I have come to you for help," Riya said softly.

"Tell me, what can I do to help you, Riya," Sheetal said, feeling genuinely sorry for her. All her negativity towards her had vanished; she was also a victim of Sanjay's selfishness, just like her.

"I don't want to be defeated without giving a fight. I can't let Sanjay go scot-free. He will use and throw another woman, Sheetal. He will wreck some other poor woman's life. He will have to pay for what he has done."

'This is no defeated woman.' Sheetal thought as she looked at the woman in front of her. 'This is a determined woman.'

"Sheetal, I want you to file a case against Sanjay. Make him pay for all the mental torture that he has made me go through. I want him punished for staying with me as my husband and discarding me when the baby died. Thanks to him, now I have no source of income. He will have to either marry me or compensate me financially."

Sheetal was shocked. She had never imagined it could be this. 'But why not?' She asked herself. 'Wasn't Riya abused and victimized? She, too, deserved justice!' Sheetal thought.

"Sheetal, I have no money to pay a lawyer. I know that you run an NGO to help women like me get justice. Sheetal, I beg you, please fight my case against Sanjay," pleaded Riya as she kneeled and tried to touch Sheetal's feet.

Sheetal jumped back. "No, please don't do this. Don't let that man rob you of your dignity too!"

To say that Sheetal was shaken was putting it mildly.

How could she fight a case against Sanjay, her husband of many years, father of her boys? How could she do that?

"Please don't reply now. Think it over. My only request is that don't think of this case as Sanjay's wife. Think of it as a woman. If you think I deserve justice, then take up my case."

Riya collected herself, this time with dignity, and slowly walked out of the door.

'When I think I am getting a grip on my life, it throws another curve!' Sheetal thought ruefully as she looked at the retreating back of the woman who had been the cause of major catastrophe in her life.

But try as she might, she could not feel anything but pity for her today. She genuinely felt sorry for her and wanted to help, but what Riya wanted from her was something that would rock her boat again!

Sanjay's affair with Riya changed her entire life, but in the end, everything turned out in her favour and for her good. Her life had meaning and a purpose now. Every morning when she got up from bed, there was a spring in her steps. At night, when her head touched the pillow, she did not worry about Sanjay or Rohit or the boys; she worried about how she would win the cases that she was fighting. She could not afford to lose, for she was not fighting for name, fame or money. She was fighting for a cause; she was fighting so that her clients could live life with dignity and without any kind of physical or emotional abuse.

In the past few months, she realised the difference between living a radar-less life and living a life with a purpose! She now realized that having a purpose in life was like having a powerful drug; you get used to having it, and life seems meaningless without it.

She had now found the meaning of her existence!

Now that she had found a balance, this again was something that would bring turmoil in her life. How could she support someone who was working against the father of her children? How would she explain that to her children?

Would she ever have a clear conscience if she chose not to help Riya? Would she be true to the cause she was fighting for? Would she not feel like a hypocrite?

She was again at crossroads, and a lot depended on which path she chose.

It felt like eons, but it was less than an hour that she had sat there, deep in contemplation. She always told her children, "Whenever in doubt, listen to your heart. The heart, though on the left, is always right." Today, when the time had come for her to decide, would she do the same?

She knew the answer. She knew the path she had to take. She was a woman fighting for a cause. She was a woman first, and she could not let down another woman. It did not matter if there were personal challenges; she would have to overcome them. She would accept Riya's case.

Dusk was falling outside, and things were not visible clearly. However, in the room, the darkness had gone and doubts had disappeared.

The doubts were replaced by determination, and she knew that however strong the storm would be, she would survive because she was a woman, and every woman is a survivor. She needs a little support sometimes, someone to hold her hand and tell her that everything would be fine. Riya needed that support, and she would not fail her. She would not fail another woman, for she was - for her!

www.ingramcontent.com/pod-product-compliance
Ingram Content Group UK Ltd.
Pitfield, Milton Keynes, MK11 3LW, UK
UKHW042001230426
12048UKWH00009B/479